William Edward Norris

The Countess Radna

A Novel. Vol. 1, Second Edition

William Edward Norris

The Countess Radna
A Novel. Vol. 1, Second Edition

ISBN/EAN: 9783337273668

Printed in Europe, USA, Canada, Australia, Japan

Cover: Foto ©Andreas Hilbeck / pixelio.de

More available books at **www.hansebooks.com**

THE

COUNTESS RADNA

A NOVEL

BY

W. E. NORRIS

AUTHOR OF 'HIS GRACE,' 'NO NEW THING,' ETC.

IN THREE VOLUMES

VOL. I.

Second   Edition

LONDON

WILLIAM HEINEMANN

1893

CONTENTS OF VOL. I.

THE COUNTESS RADNA

CHAPTER I.

THE HERO MEETS THE HEROINE.

' COLBORNE — Douglas Colborne?' said his Excellency the British Ambassador to the French Republic. 'No; I don't remember ever to have heard of him before; still, that is no fault of his, and I dare say he is all right. Even if he isn't all right, it doesn't much matter. By all means ask him to your horrid crush!'

Lady Royston, the Ambassador's wife, who was seated at her writing-table, was a tall, graceful woman, not so very many years younger than her gray-headed little husband as she looked.

' I was wondering,' said she, ' whether we

ought not, perhaps, to ask him to dinner. He called yesterday and left a letter of introduction from Peggy Rowley. She says——'

'Oh,' interrupted Sir Edmund Royston, with a laugh, 'what she says is of no consequence. From the moment that Peg Rowley answers for him, we are bound to accept him. Tell her, with my love, that her friend shall be looked after and that everything shall be done to make his stay in Paris pleasant. That is, unless he is an inquiring M.P. or a man with ideas about European politics who writes for reviews—in either of which cases you will have to undertake him. You might intimate to Peg that it is as much as my place is worth to mix myself up with people of that kind, and that I really can't do it, even to please her.'

But Mr. Colborne, it appeared, was not a person of that kind. After her husband had left her, Lady Royston glanced again at the open letter which lay before her, and which seemed to classify the stranger in a few graphic touches :

'I hope you will be kind to him, and introduce him to anybody worth knowing ; for he rather requires introductions to those

who are worth knowing, having hitherto led
the healthy but narrow sort of life that most
young Englishmen of good birth lead. They
are sure to like him, and so are you ; because
he is very nice in every way. Clever, too,
and with distinct ambitions—which isn't a
disadvantage. His mother considers him
remarkably good - looking, and there are
moments when I almost agree with her. At
any rate, he has good manners, and he has
lately succeeded to a property near this which
ought to be worth more than it is, and he
has resigned his commission in the Guards in
order to look after it, and I shouldn't wonder
if he were to get into Parliament one of these
days—and I believe that is about all. Don't
cold-shoulder him. You will hurt his feelings if you do, not to speak of mine ; for I
am fond of his mother and his sisters, and I
want him to be a credit to them. He can't
be expected to do credit to anybody or anything until he has seen a little more of the
world than he has at present.'

After that, the very least that Lady Royston could do was to take care that a card of
invitation to her forthcoming reception should
be despatched to Mr. Colborne's hotel. She

thought it might be as well just to have a
look at him before taking further steps ;
because in these days the utmost circumspec-
tion is, unhappily, necessary, and it can no
longer be deemed an absolute guarantee of
fitness for the highest circles to have held a
commission in the Guards, or even to be a
friend and neighbour of Peggy Rowley's.

However, the misgivings of this experienced
lady were satisfactorily dispelled before she
had exchanged a dozen observations with the
hero of the present narrative. Douglas Colborne, it may at once be stated, is only presented to the reader as a hero in the sense of
having been the chief personage affected by
certain events and episodes : nobody has ever
thought of calling him heroic, nor, if there
was a substratum of heroism in his character, was it of that nature which appeals
to popular enthusiasm and is rewarded by
laurel wreaths. But everybody who knew
him admitted that he was a thorough gentleman, and Lady Royston, without knowing
him at all, admitted as much as soon
as she saw him and heard his voice. He
approached her on the evening of her reception, threading his way through the gold-

laced and ribboned official throng which had congregated near the doorway, with the easy, assured air of one who knows that he is in his proper place, and is consequently free from any embarrassing consciousness of his own personality. He was a tall, spare young man, with dark hair and iron-gray eyes, not exactly handsome, yet as near being so as any male specimen of the race can be required to be, and his clothes fitted well, and he had a pleasant, honest sort of smile. He shook hands with his hostess, and, as in duty bound, said something about their common friend, Miss Rowley; after which Lady Royston inquired whether he had come to Paris for any special purpose, or merely as a tourist.

'Oh, I'm a mere tourist,' he answered, laughing. 'I haven't many ideas as yet, and I haven't come here in search of them, though, of course, I shouldn't mind picking up any that might be going. It was Miss Rowley who urged me to cross the Channel by way of widening my mental horizon. She has an impression—I'm sure I don't know whether it is a correct one or not—that Paris is the centre of modern civilization.'

'That is the usual impression,' Lady Royston

observed. 'Most likely Peggy is right, for she almost always is, and I suppose there can be no doubt that society is rather more cosmopolitan here than it is in London ; but I can't speak from personal knowledge, because I am not allowed to make acquaintance with people, I am only allowed to look at them. You would like to make acquaintance with them, perhaps ?'

'Well, yes,' replied the young man ; ' I think I should—if they are worth the trouble.'

'Some of them are. There is the Countess Radna, for instance, who is quite cosmopolitan. She is the most beautiful woman I have ever seen in my life, besides being fabulously rich, absolutely independent and rather eccentric. She delights in new types, I am told, and probably you would strike her as a new type, though I won't promise that she shall be delighted with you. Would you care to take the chance ?'

To such an invitation only one response was possible, and Douglas Colborne made it with the more alacrity because he was eager to see with his own eyes and hear with his own ears what foreigners (he did not imagine that there was any very important difference

between one kind of foreigner and another)
were like when you came to talk to them.
Presently, therefore, he was making his best
bow to the most beautiful woman Lady
Royston had ever seen in her life.

Was she the most beautiful woman he had
ever seen in the course of his more limited
experience ?   He really thought that she
was ; certainly, she was not at all like the
rest of the world.   Her wavy brown hair was
drawn up and back from her low, broad fore-
head ; her eyes were of that dark blue colour
which is rarely seen out of Ireland ; her
complexion was almost unnaturally perfect
(though the credit of having produced it
belonged to Nature alone) ; her little straight
nose, her short upper lip, and her rounded
chin proclaimed the nobility of her birth, as
did also the poise of her head and the grace
of her movements.   She had some diamonds
of great size round her neck and in her hair,
otherwise her costume was simple enough—
or, at all events, it appeared so to him.   She
reminded him of certain miniatures, representing beauties of the last century, which he had
always hitherto set down as over-flattering to
the deceased ladies.   It now seemed quite

upon the cards that the Countess Radna's great-grandmother might have been accurately portrayed by one of them. Having met nobody at all resembling her before, he naturally did not know what to make of her; but she, apparently, was troubled by no such difficulty as regarded him, for after a rapid survey of his person, she asked, with a smile, and without a trace of accent :

' Oxford or Cambridge ?'

' Well, if you put it in that way, Oxford,' he replied. ' Nevertheless, I took my degree nearly three years ago. Do I look so very juvenile ?'

She shrugged her shoulders slightly.

' It is the most excusable of all defects, and, such as it is, you will not suffer from it long enough to find it wearisome. Three years ago, you say ? And since then ?'

' Since then I have been a sort of a soldier, and now I am nothing at all, except a country gentleman in a humble way. But I dare say you don't know what that means.'

' Not very distinctly, because I have never been in England, but I have met many Englishmen and read innumerable books about your island. I think I can guess what a country gentleman is. As a general rule, he needs some other vocation than that, does he not? You have come to Paris to seek for one, perhaps?'

'No; only to divert myself, and to pick up stray scraps of information and experience. I brought a letter of introduction to Lady Royston, who, as you see, is passing me on to her friends. So much the worse for her friends, you will say.'

'Why should I say so? On the contrary, I congratulate myself upon the honour of being included among Lady Royston's friends. Do you speak French at all?'

'Only when I can't help it; but I understand what is said to me.'

'Then you are more fortunate than I am. I very often fail to understand what is said to me; but I am too good a linguist to refrain from talking when I should do better to hold my tongue. I asked the question because I was wondering whether, if you are disengaged, you would care to dine with me to-morrow evening and meet a few celebrities. They are famous without deserving fame, most of them; still, they are amusing in their way, and, as they would a great deal rather entertain you than be entertained by you, you won't have to exert yourself if you come.'

Mr. Colborne accepted the invitation unhesitatingly, and was endeavouring to express his gratitude in fitting terms, when she interrupted him rather brusquely by saying, ' Very well ; eight o'clock, then. Avenue Friedland —every cab-driver in Paris knows the house.'

' So that you yourself are quite as celebrated as your guests, I suppose?'

' Oh, I suppose so. Paris is a small place —much smaller than London ; and I am a big personage—much bigger than I look. Everybody will tell you that, if you will make inquiries ; only they won't be able to tell you why I am big, because neither they nor I know. Probably it is because I am considered odd, and because oddity is fashionable.'

He would have liked to ask her in what her oddity consisted, but she gave him no opportunity of prosecuting his researches, for she now turned away to speak to one of the high official gentlemen who had been hovering near her during the above colloquy, and he was fain to apply for further information to a second Secretary of Embassy, Lindsay by name, with whom he had some slight acquaintance. Mr. Lindsay knew all about the Countess Radna, and was willing to tell all that he knew.

'She is an heiress of the very first water,' said he, 'one of those heiresses who can't be produced out of the Austro - Hungarian Empire, and aren't produced very freely there, because, as a general rule, Hungarian counts, like other people, manage to have sons. The late Count Radna didn't manage to accomplish that feat, and the consequence is that the lady who has asked you to dinner —it isn't everybody whom she asks to dinner, let me tell you—has larger estates and a vast deal more money than the common run of European royalties. Odd? Oh, well, I don't know that there is anything particularly odd about her, except that she is still single and that it isn't over and above easy to get even with her. Of course she gives herself airs— any woman in her position and with her face would—but she hasn't earned a character for being specially *émancipée* so far. However, I can't pretend to be among her intimates. I have known her ever since she came to Paris, about six months ago, but she hasn't asked me to dine yet, and I imagine that she never

will.   What made her ask *you* to dine, do you
suppose ?'

Douglas Colborne was quite unable to say.
He deemed it probable that he owed the
honour conferred upon him to his obscurity ;
but this suggestion was scouted by the young
diplomatist, who assured him that the
Countess had no fancy for ciphers.

' Then,' said he, ' perhaps she asked me
because she has a fancy for new types.   Lady
Royston told me that she had, and thought I
might present myself to her in the light of
one.'

' Ah, yes, that may be,' agreed Mr. Lindsay,
whose vanity may have been soothed by the
hypothesis ; ' yes, you would naturally strike
her as being rather raw.   Which you are, you
know, if you'll excuse my saying so.   From
her point of view, I mean.'

Douglas Colborne did not at all mind being
considered raw from anybody's point of view.
He was not conceited, and was well aware
that he had as yet seen only a very small part
of the very small planet which we inhabit.
He was anxious to see as much more of it as
he could before finally settling down into the
narrow channel marked out for him by

destiny ; and that was one reason why he looked forward with pleasure and curiosity to the entertainment to which he had been bidden. Another was that he had been greatly attracted by the Countess Radna's beauty, as well as by the informality of her manner.

Yet she was formal enough when he presented himself, at the appointed hour, at her hôtel in the Avenue Friedland, and when she rose to receive him. She briefly introduced him to three or four of his fellow-guests (he noticed that before doing so she had to consult some ivory tablets, attached to her fan, in order to make sure of his name), and then resumed her seat and her conversation with an old gentleman whom he afterwards discovered to be one of the most famous of modern French painters. This indifference chilled him a little, as it may not impossibly have been intended to do ; but he enjoyed the evening in spite of it. There were sixteen people present, and a dozen of them were what she had promised they should be, celebrities. Whether she had accurately described some of them as being famous without having deserved fame, Douglas Colborne did not presume to judge ; but after a time he thought her amply justified in having called them amusing. He was placed at the dinner-table between two ladies, one of whom was the wife of a Minister, while the other, who was a widow, was known to all Europe as a Legitimist, an ardent sportswoman and a politician (as far as the providing of funds went) for the fun of the thing. Understanding enough of French to follow a comedy at the Théâtre Français, he did not understand the language quite sufficiently to appreciate all its recent developments, so that he missed some of the amenities which were exchanged across him between this couple of fair antagonists ; still, he caught a few of them, and was diverted by them ; he himself was scarcely required to open his lips ; and when, from time to time, he took the liberty of listening to the incessant and rather noisy conversation which was being carried on at a greater distance from him, he found that also extremely diverting. If the Countess Radna was odd in nothing else, she was evidently odd in her selection of those whom it pleased her to assemble under her roof. It was not necessary to possess any intimate knowledge of Parisian society in order to perceive that she had collected what Mr. Colborne mentally characterized as ' a mixed pack,' nor could it be doubted that a world-renowned philosopher and freethinker, an ascetic bishop, an ex-diplomatist of the Second Empire, and a former member of the Provisional Government of 1870 had been invited to meet one another for experimental and slightly mischievous purposes. They did not, however, come to blows, and their hostess apparently derived less satisfaction from their wordy altercations, their sarcasms and their witticisms, than the young Englishman who was watching her did. He noticed that she ate scarcely anything and spoke very little. Most of the time she was leaning back in her chair, fanning herself languidly and looking most unaffectedly bored, and once, when their eyes chanced to meet, she made a little depre-catory grimace at him, as who should say : ' After all, it wasn't worth your while to come, was it ? The puppets won't dance.'

For his part, he thought that they were dancing quite creditably, and later in the evening he made so bold as to take advantage of an opportunity for telling her so much. After dinner the company adjourned to a conservatory, where coffee and liqueurs and cigarettes were served ; and espying a vacant chair at his hostess's elbow, he audaciously possessed himself of it.

' *Tant mieux !*' said she. in answer to his observation ; ' since you are amused, there is no need for me to apologize. Nevertheless, they are not amusing. They might be if they believed in themselves, or their theories, or their principles ; but the unfortunate thing is that not one of them, unless perhaps it may be the old bishop, does. Are you, by any chance, provided with a creed, political, social, or religious, which you take seriously ? If you were, one would be grateful to you for proclaiming it.'

' Oh, I suppose I am,' answered the young man, laughing. ' I believe in Christianity and the political supremacy of the landed classes. Also, to a great extent, in human nature and in the perfectibility of the species.'

' What droll articles of faith ! I don't see how you can make the first agree with the residue ; but if you really believe in the last, you must believe that one man is as good as another.'

' Oh dear no ; if anything is patent to the

meanest capacity, it is that the intelligent minority always must and will govern the stupid majority, whether your form of government be monarchical or republican.'

' And universal suffrage ?'

'Well, we know how that works. Of course, it is an idiotic system; but it admits of manipulation and is manipulated. Put it how you will, our only concern is to secure a majority of the minority, and we could do it in England if only the Radicals were not so abominably unscrupulous. It is different in foreign countries, because you have the fear of war constantly before your eyes ; and although you may enjoy worrying the men who hold office, you wouldn't like to throw them over and put the Socialists into the saddle.'

The Countess was perhaps more interested in her interlocutor's personality than in his political views. She made no response to these; but presently she said :

' You are actually and seriously a Christian, then ?'

'Certainly I am. Aren't you ?'

'No ; I have passed through that phase, and have had to abandon the theory, not without regret. It is a pretty theory ; but unluckily it isn't true—at all events, it can't be proved to be true.'

' Oh, if you insist upon proofs——'

' Isn't that just what one has a right to insist upon, supposing that one possesses any rights at all ? What right, I wonder, have I to be enjoying every luxury that money can buy, while hundreds of thousands of my fellow-creatures haven't enough to eat ?'

' Have you any inclination to resign your privileges ?'

' Not the smallest. Only, if the populace were to deprive me of them some fine day, I shouldn't have the effrontery to complain ; all I could do would be to protest that I had been born, through no fault of my own, to my present position in the world, which I had no hand in bringing to its present pass. The truly consolatory and delightful thing would be to believe, as I suppose you do, that we are all where we are and what we are by the decree of some wise and supernatural Creator. It would be a funny belief to hold, no doubt ; but it isn't in the least funny to hold no belief, and it is most particularly stupid to profess a belief which one doesn't really hold.

That is why everybody, except you, is so particularly stupid this evening.'

The young Englishman said he was glad to hear that he was exceptional, although he had never expected to be so styled in virtue of his being obviously ordinary.

'You seem to have gone so far in your search for abnormal beings,' he remarked, 'that an encounter with a normal Briton is quite a pleasant shock and surprise to you.'

'Who told you that I was in search of abnormal beings?' retorted the Countess. 'Don't try to say clever things ; that is not at all the *rôle* of the normal Briton, and you are not likely to shine in it. You will probably shine in other ways before long, if you continue to be simple and honest ; only you should beware of sneering at what seems to you to be morbid affectation. We are morbid, I confess ; but we are not affected, and, such as we are, we constitute the majority of the minority that you were speaking about just now. You will have to reckon with us when you have attained the summit of your ambition, and been invited to take your place as one of your Queen's advisers. That is, if your minority is worth considering at all—as

I dare say it may be for another half-century. Let us talk about something else now.'

However, she did not seem very eager to talk about anything else ; for she soon rose, and, crossing the room, seated herself beside the artist, who was possibly more successful in amusing her than Douglas Colborne had been. The latter took his leave with a regretful impression that he had affronted his hostess, and a strong desire to see more of her. He was youthful enough to be ignorant of the essential characteristics of the opposite sex ; he was clever enough to have half divined the necessity of keeping women (for their own sakes) in a state of subjection, and he was sensitive enough to have been slightly piqued by a display of that very ancient recipe of theirs for temporarily subjugating their natural masters. Once give a young man to understand that he has inspired you with a certain amused, disdainful liking, as for a worthy, inexperienced sort of creature, and if, after that, you cannot get him to fall in love with you, you must be possessed of physical advantages far inferior to those of which the Countess Radna could boast.

Not, of course, that Douglas Colborne had the remotest intention or idea of falling in love with this fair and wealthy Hungarian. He had a cool head on his shoulders, and he knew very well that he could no more aspire to ally himself with a grandee of that class than with a Royal Highness. Besides, he did not mean to marry anybody for a good many years to come. For a good many years to come he would have plenty to do and think about. He had to get a neglected property into order, if that could be done ; he had to carve out some sort of a career for himself ; he had also to look after his mother and sisters, who might not improbably require looking after. Nevertheless, he thought that the Countess Radna might be cured of the erroneous ideas she had taken up ; in addition to which, he felt sure that she was really worth far more than she chose to represent herself as being. In addition to that, again, he rendered a just and dispassionate tribute to the loveliness of her person, which made her mere presence a boon to the just and dispassionate critic. Musing thus over a nocturnal cigar after he had returned to his hotel, he resolved that he would call upon her on the following Thursday. She had mentioned to him, when he took leave of her, that she was at home on Thursdays.

CHAPTER II.

IF we all of us had everything that we could wish for, how miserable we should all be ! That is what has been impressed upon us, without convincing us, by innumerable philosophers and divines, ever since those two classes of more or less useful mortals sprang into existence to meet as well as they could, with their wise platitudes, the demands of a dissatisfied race. However, if there is one thing more certain than another, it is that the most fortunate of us may always rely upon having something still remaining to long for ; and it was owing to the above happy provision on the part of nature that the Countess Radna was not really quite as miserable as she thought herself. It is true that she had vast wealth, rare beauty, absolute independence,

and health so excellent that there was not the
slightest need for the services of the physician
who formed one of her household ; yet it was
a matter of no difficulty whatsoever to her to
be depressed and discontented, while nothing
debarred her from the consolation of believing
that she would have been a hundred thousand
times better off if she had been somebody else.
Although it is doubtful whether she would
have enjoyed washing clothes and cleaning
grates, she often envied washerwomen and
housemaids, whose duties are obvious, whose
work must be done, whether they are in the
mood for it or not, and who have no leisure to
sit down and meditate ruefully upon the dreadful, dreary monotony of life. The Countess
Radna was four-and-twenty years of age—not
less than that—her parents had died during
her childhood ; she had long been released
from the supervision of her guardians ; she
had been everywhere, she had seen everything, and she would willingly have written
an additional chapter to the Book of Eccle-
siastes had she been possessed of the requisite
skill.

The worst of it was that she possessed
no skill, literary or other ; at any rate, this

was what she said to herself in her frequent
moments of despondency. She could paint a
little; she could play the piano a little; she
had read rather more, and she could, when
she chose to take trouble, talk a good deal
better than most women; but what was the
good of all that? What was the good of
owning large tracts of country to which you
couldn't pay more than a flying visit without
being tempted to cut your throat? What was
the good of wandering about Europe, if you
could only look forward to meeting the same
dull people over and over again? What was
the good of being courted and admired, unless
you could bring yourself to feel some vestige
of admiration for your admirers? What,
indeed, was the good of being alive, since existence appeared to be merely synonymous
with weariness and disgust? One fine morning the Countess put some of these cheerful
questions—not for the first time—to her body
physician, Dr. Schott, who chuckled in his
gray beard, shook his fat sides, and prescribed
a tonic. Dr. Schott had an easy and well-
paid berth, which he probably was not anxious
to relinquish. He had always assured his
gracious mistress that her constitution was a

frail one ; but having a tolerably clear comprehension of her character, he had been careful to refrain from vexing her by subserviency
of manner, nor had he ever scrupled to
laugh at her fancies and her continual trifling
ailments.

'A few grains of quinine are very well,'
said he ; 'change of scene would be better ;
but what would be best of all would be to get
up an interest in something or somebody—
especially somebody. When one is interested
in what is outside, one forgets to think about
what is within.'

'I ask nothing better,' returned the
Countess. 'Will you be so good as to provide me with somebody in whom it is possible
to take an interest ? If you can discover such
a person in Paris, you will be more fortunate
than I have been, so far. To be sure, I remember now that there is a young Englishman
who dined here the other night, and who
seemed to me to differ in some ways from
the rest of the nobodies. Come to my reception this afternoon, and tell me what you
think of him. He is almost certain to call.'

'A fresh *brétendant?*' inquired the Doctor,
with his thick, Teutonic laugh.

'No, not a *prétendant*; and I wish you
would not use French words, dear doctor—
your pronunciation of them gets upon my
nerves. He is a sort of schoolboy ; but he is
fresh, and, after a fashion, original, and I liked
him. You shall tell me whether he is going
to be a man or not some day—you who are so
clever at reading character.'

The Doctor was really a very fair judge of
ordinary character ; but as much could hardly
be said for the Baroness von Bickenbach, who
ranked next to him in the Countess Radna's
household, and whom that lady now proceeded
to summon to her presence.

' Bickenbach,' said she, when the faded little
middle-aged woman who had once been her
governess, and who was now utilized by her
in the alternative capacities of housekeeper,
chaperon and companion, had appeared in
prompt obedience to her commands, ' if you
had nothing better to do, it would be kind
of you to help me out with the entertainment
of the host of tiresome people who may be
expected to invade the house this afternoon.'

' Ach, most gracious Countess !' sighed the
other, ' you know that your wishes are my

law ; but you know also that I am not entertaining.'

'Possibly not to them ; yet you never fail
to entertain me by the things that you say
about them after they are gone away. Keep
your eye upon a young Englishman of the
name of Colborne, my good Bickenbach, and
when you have studied him, let me hear what
impression he has produced upon you. It
has been his great privilege to please me :
isn't he a fortunate man ?'

The Baroness thought him fortunate indeed,
and expressed her opinion with the utmost
emphasis. Furthermore, she was very anxious
to learn whether the favoured Englishman
was handsome, and whether he belonged to
what she was pleased to call *la haute volée*.
Like Dr. Schott, she was always expecting
the advent of the man upon whom the control
of her patroness's fortune must some day
devolve ; but, unlike him, she was free from
any selfish prejudices in the matter. She was
romantic, as the ladies of her nation commonly
are ; she desired, above all things, that her
beloved Countess Hélène should be happy ;
she had a firm faith in the possibility of
matrimonial felicity, and as for herself, her

little economies enabled her to look forward
with comparative equanimity to the not improbable event of her dismissal. But this
legitimate curiosity on her part received
scant gratification; for her beloved Countess
Hélène only answered:

‘Bickenbach, you bore me. There is just
a chance—but I am afraid it is a poor one—
that Mr. Colborne may amuse me for a short
time; he is not an Adonis, and it would
make no difference to me if he were. You
ought to understand me well enough to know
that, if I every marry at all, I shall marry
somebody of whom I am a little afraid. One
is not afraid of students and *débutants*, and
one doesn't take the trouble to notice their
features or inquire who their fathers may be.’

Notwithstanding this contemptuous declaration, the Countess Radna had deigned to
notice that Douglas Colborne was a pleasant,
manly-looking young fellow, and when, in
accordance with her anticipations, he entered
her drawing-room that afternoon amongst
other visitors, she did think it worth while
to question him upon the subject of his
parentage. On being informed that his father
was dead, that he was his own master, that

he had no other near relations than a mother
and two sisters, and that his modest mansion,
with the adjacent lands, had been the property of his family for a matter of three
centuries, she remarked :

'That is as much as to say that your
position has been created for you, and that
the only problem you have to solve is how to
get through your life without becoming sick
of it.'

'Oh, I am not so hard up for problems as
that,' he replied, with a laugh ; 'there are
plenty of others which will take me all my
time to solve, I expect. How to pay my way
will be one of them, and my people think that
how to get into Parliament ought to be a
second. Not that I should be in any danger
of becoming sick of life, even if I were a
county member already and as rich as a
Rothschild. Such as they are, the amusements of life are quite good enough for me.'

'You mean, perhaps, what you and your
compatriots call sport—hunting and shooting ?'

'Yes ; and games. Luckily for me, I love
games. I love hunting and shooting, and
racing, too ; but I can't expect to have the

cream of these things, because I can't afford
them. Still, one can treat one's self to the
pleasure of looking on at some of them, and I
mean to look on at the Grand Prix next
Sunday, though it does take place on an un-
lawful day. Shall you be there ?'

' *C'est selon :* I shall be there if I am in a
mood to go there when the time comes ;
but I am deprived of the temptation which
you enjoy, because the only difference that
I can discern between Sunday and Monday is that Monday will bring me twenty-
four hours nearer to the end of this tedious
comedy or tragedy — whichever it may
be. So you actually believe that you will
commit a sin by attending a race-meeting on
the first day of the week, and you mean to
attend it in spite of your belief ? Happy
man !'

Mr. Colborne explained. He did not deem
it a sin to be present at the Grand Prix—
otherwise he would deny himself that pleasure
—but in England there were still to be found
thousands of excellent people who held that
strict obedience to the Ten Commandments, as
adapted to the requirements of modern English life, was essential ; so that if, by an im-

possibility, such a thing as a Sunday race-meeting were to be proposed in his native land, he should feel bound to discountenance it.

' I don't feel bound,' he added, ' to insist upon the observance of the Jewish Sabbath ; nobody does observe it, and nobody dreams of doing so. Still, some concessions must be made to inherited prejudices, and it is better, after all, that the masses should stick to an exaggerated creed than that they should abandon everything in the shape of a creed. Don't you think so ?'

' Infinitely better,' she answered, ' and so the French nation will discover before the twentieth century begins. It is also very wise on the part of the instructed few to pander to the prejudices of the uninstructed many. Whether it is quite honest is another question ; but that concerns you more than me. Anyhow, I may look forward to the felicity of seeing you at Longchamps, and perhaps, if I do, you will kindly try to enlighten me as to the excitement that can be derived from ascertaining that this long-legged, narrow-chested horse can get over a given space of ground in a slightly shorter time than that.'

Douglas Colborne had a great deal to say in reply to so absurd a travesty of the signification of horse-racing ; but she did not listen to him very attentively, and her next remark was totally irrelevant.

'You talk with an authoritative accent,' said she ; 'it seems a pity that you should no longer be a soldier, because fighting is the one clear and satisfactory business that remains open to men in these days. Although, as far as one can see at present, it would have taken you rather more than an average lifetime to have become a Field-Marshal. Do you never sigh for military glory ? You look as if you ought to.'

'It is my humble endeavour to sigh for nothing that I can't possibly have,' he answered, laughing. 'Meanwhile, I have just been made a Colonel of Yeomanry ; so that when our friends on this side of the Channel become our enemies and invade us, they will find me ready to receive them at the head of the distinguished corps which I command.'

She shrugged her shoulders.

'Did I not tell you that you were a happy man !' she exclaimed. 'Imagine one whose ambition it is to desire only what he can get !

I really must introduce you to Dr. Schott,
who will cordially sympathize with you, and
to my companion, the Baroness von Bickenbach, who shares your ideas without having
the faintest suspicion that she shares them.
Don't make fun of Bickenbach, unless you
wish to hurt my feelings. You will think her
a fool ; but she is not a fool, because nobody
who is so perfectly sincere can be.'

It was little that Douglas Colborne cared
whether the clumsy, colourless German *frau*
to whom he was presented was as wise as
Solomon or as silly as she presented every
appearance of being. He did not want to
talk to her or to Dr. Schott, and he would
have liked very much to talk a little longer
with his hostess. But the latter had either
had enough of him or thought that the rest of
her visitors had not had quite enough of her ;
for she now turned away, and during the next
quarter of an hour it devolved upon him to
make conversation for the benefit of her
dependents. He got on pretty well with the
Baroness, who entertained him with extravagant eulogies of her former pupil and present
mistress, extolling the Countess Radna's kindness of heart and boundless liberality, while

she deplored the influence of the *Zeitgeist*,
which, according to her, led so many pure
and noble beings into representing themselves
as something infinitely inferior to what they
actually were.   The Baroness might be foolish,
but seemed to be sympathetic ; whereas Dr.
Schott displayed none of the sympathy and
cordiality with which he had been credited in
advance.   Dr. Schott was somewhat grumpy
and surly ; Dr. Schott, to tell the truth, had
taken the stranger's measure, and had been
dissatisfied with the result of his scrutiny.
' Young, not ill-looking, rather clever than
stupid, and remarkably fresh,' was the
Doctor's inward verdict. ' Just the sort of
fellow to captivate her, and just the sort of
fellow to make the position of resident
physician uncomfortable. *Das geht nicht!*'
Consequently, Schott said some rather rude
things about the importance of England as a
factor in European politics. He was very
well aware that nothing that he could say or
do would interfere with the gratification of
his mistress's caprices ; but that knowledge
left him free to indulge his own ill-humour,
and he did not deny himself so modest a
luxury.

When Mr. Colborne took leave of the Countess he made so bold as to inquire why she kept a tame doctor. 'And not such a very tame one either, if it comes to that,' he remarked. 'Your doctor growls and shows his teeth even while one is patting him on the head and saying nice things to him.'

'Does he?' she returned, laughing. 'Well, that shows what a capital watch-dog he is. I am sorry if he growled at you ; but perhaps that may have been because you couldn't distinguish his head from his tail, and stroked him the wrong way. I have known such mistakes made by others before now ; still, I have very seldom met with anybody who could manage to irritate my dear, good Bickenbach. I trust you haven't been laughing at her.'

'Not for one moment. She has been praising you up to the skies, and there was nothing to laugh at in that.'

The Countess gave him a smiling little bow of acknowledgment and dismissal. She herself affected a *sans façon* which bordered upon familiarity ; but her rank and her wealth placed her upon so lofty an eminence that she was little accustomed to familiarity on the part of her associates, and the simple, self-possessed manners of this young Englishman tickled without offending her.

'Many thanks,' she interrupted her esteemed physician and counsellor by saying, after the company had departed, 'but, upon second thoughts, I am not sure that I care to hear your opinion of Mr. Colborne. I have formed my own, and it is a favourable one.'

Bickenbach made a soft murmur of assent, while Dr. Schott returned roughly, 'You will change your opinion, or else you will be sorry for not having changed it.'

Thereupon the Countess threw herself back in her chair, and laughed heartily. The thinly-veiled apprehensions of the Doctor always made her laugh, and she was always careful to refrain from reassuring him. He would have been far less diverting than he was had it been in his power to discern the absurdity of imagining that she, who had refused countless brilliant alliances, was likely to bestow her hand or her affections upon an obscure young Briton.

CHAPTER III.

On the following day Douglas Colborne did his duty by calling at the British Embassy. Lady Royston was at home, and made herself extremely pleasant, hoping that he would not scruple to make use of her during his sojourn in Paris, and that if there was anybody in particular whom he would like to meet he would let her know.

'For my own part,' she remarked, 'I am too good an Englishwoman to appreciate the society of other nations; still, no doubt it does one good to rub shoulders with them from time to time. It's a wholesome sort of alterative.'

He thanked her, but said that he had hardly had time as yet to assimilate the dose with which she had already been kind enough to provide him. 'The Countess Radna,' he observed, 'is a tremendous alterative.'

'Is she ? Well, I dare say you know her better than I do, for you have been to dinner with her, I hear. When she speaks to me she talks like anybody else ; but that may be because I am only a woman. Men, I believe, become crazy about her, and one can't wonder at it, considering how lovely she is. Nevertheless, I wouldn't imitate them in that respect if I were you. In fact, I must beg as a personal favour that you won't, because if you did I should get into trouble with Peggy Rowley, of whom, I may confess to you in strict confidence, I am a good deal frightened.'

Colborne laughed at the idea of anybody being afraid of Peg Rowley, whom he had known intimately from his earliest childhood, and who did not strike him as a formidable personage ; but he declared that he was in no peril of losing his heart to the fascinating Countess.

'I know my place,' said he, 'and I fully realize what a great gulf is fixed between an English country gentleman on a small scale and a Hungarian magnate. Yet I must say that I should like to make friends with her, especially as she seems quite disposed to be friendly. At all events, she is very candid. She told me one or two things about herself which made me feel rather sorry for her.'

' That does credit to the tenderness of your heart, though I should think you might easily discover some more deserving subject for pity.'

' Oh, one can't tell; beauty and riches aren't everything. Anyhow, I hope I shall find out a little more about her before I take leave of her for ever, and I am in hopes of encountering her at the Grand Prix on Sunday. Do you propose to honour the races by your presence ?'

The Ambassadress shook her head; there were a great many things which she was not permitted to do, she informed him, and Sir Edmund Royston thought that going to the races on Sunday ought to be one of them. ' But he doesn't ask the young men how they employ their time on that day,' she added, ' and I suspect that your friend Mr. Lindsay will make a point of being at Longchamps. You had better get him to take you with him ; he is very well qualified to act as a cicerone.'

Mr. Colborne thought this was not a bad suggestion, and, looking in at the Chancery afterwards, obtained a prompt offer of a seat in the second secretary's dog-cart for the occasion. In the plenitude of his hospitality Mr. Lindsay offered furthermore to back the favourite on his behalf ; but he declined to risk his money, alleging that he was, for once, more anxious to see the spectators than the sport.

'Well, they're worth looking at, some of them,' returned the other, and proceeded to mention a few of the ladies who appeared to him worthy of an inquiring stranger's notice.

'Oh, I don't mean women of that sort,' returned Colborne, with a slight gesture of disgust ; ' I mean high society in general, and the Countess Radna in particular.'

'That's it, is it?' exclaimed Lindsay, raising his eyebrows. ' You have made the most of your time, it seems. Did she give you a rendezvous, if one may venture to ask ?'

' Of course not; but she said there was a chance of her being there.'

' Then the odds are that she won't be there, and it's still longer odds that if she is there she won't speak to you. From what I have heard of the lady, that's her little way—an old dodge, you know, but usually an effective one. Don't blame me when she cuts you dead, that's all.'

Colborne replied, laughing, that he would blame nobody for the occurrence of such a calamity—not even the Countess Radna herself, who, supposing that she did cut him, would certainly do so only because she had failed to recognise him, not because she had deemed it worth her while to employ any dodges, old or new, for his subjugation.

But this becoming modesty did not prevent him from being a little bit disappointed and a little bit mortified by the verification of Mr. Lindsay's prophecy. The Countess Radna did attend the meeting ; he saw her from afar in a stand to which he was doubtful whether he could obtain admittance, surrounded by a crowd of individuals of whom the greater part wore uniforms and decorations ; but all he got from her was one of those vague smiling bows whereby it is the custom of her sex to acknowledge the salutes of casual acquaintances, and the victory of the French horse, Stuart, neither aroused his enthusiasm nor

abased his patriotic pride. What the deuce
did it matter which horse won? He was
entitled to that inward ejaculation because
he had openly avowed that he was not at
Longchamps for the sake of sport. Very
different and much more satisfactory was the
case of Mr. Lindsay, who had backed the
winner and was proportionately jubilant.

'The best colt of the year,' said he, as he
climbed up into his dog-cart and took the
reins, preparatory to driving his friend home.
'I knew that weeks ago, and all these fellows
might have known it if they had had the sense
to keep their eyes open. Well, that puts me
a couple of hundred to the good, which is
better than nothing, though I'm sorry it isn't
more. What have you been doing with
yourself all this time? Sloping about and
studying beauty and fashion, eh? I'm afraid
you must have had rather a slow day of
it.'

'I didn't expect to have an exciting day,'
answered Colborne somewhat gloomily. 'Of
course, I don't know any of these people.'

'What about your Countess, by the way?
She was there, for I caught a glimpse of her,
looking, as usual, as if she wished herself

anywhere else. Was she graciously pleased
to notice your worship's presence ?'

Colborne had to admit that her recognition
of that circumstance had been of the slightest
possible kind, whereupon his companion
laughed aloud. ' I told you how it would be,'
said he. ' If you feel any little premonitory
symptoms of a weakness in that quarter, be
advised by me, my dear boy, and stamp them
out. Really, when you come to think of it,
what conceivable comfort is there to be
obtained out of playing tame cat to one of
these magnificent ladies ? They like to keep
a stock of tame cats, and small blame to them;
but it's no part of your duty or mine to gratify
their tastes, and, luckily for us, we are not
restricted, as they are, to one solitary form of
amusement.'

No adequate reply could be made to so
sensible and succinct a summing-up of the
case, nor was any forthcoming ; but its own
inherent inadequacy was made manifest before
Mr. Lindsay's high-stepping horse had trotted
quite as far as the Arc de Triomphe. For
that showy animal had not reached the turn
out of the Avenue du Bois de Boulogne when
he was passed with very great ease by a pair

of grays, drawing a victoria in which a single lady was seated ; and presently this equipage was brought to a standstill, while a resplendent *chasseur* in a cocked hat and feathers descended from the box and approached the dog-cart, with a request from the Countess Radna that Mr. Colborne would speak to her for one moment.

Mr. Colborne, it need scarcely be said, lost no time in obeying the Countess's summons, and was rather surprised to find that, after all, she had nothing of any importance to say to him.

'I only wanted to tell you,' was her greeting, 'that I shall not be beguiled by you a second time into looking on at one of these senseless contests. The betting is the only thing that enlivens them, and if one stayed at home and backed one fly against another upon a window-pane, one would be spared the discomfort of swallowing huge mouthfuls of dust.'

'Oh, there is a great deal more in horse-racing than that,' answered Colborne. 'I could have explained to you where the difference comes in if you had allowed me the chance. But you wouldn't.'

'Ought I to have beckoned to you?' she asked, laughing. 'I am very sorry that I didn't happen to think of doing so ; because it is just possible that, if I had, you might have made this dreary day a shade less dreary for me. However, there is one thing to be said in favour of to-day, which is that it is nearly over, and to-morrow, if only the sun shines, may take away the taste of it. To-morrow my good Bickenbach and I are going into the country, all by ourselves, to look at green fields and gather wild-flowers and forget what sophisticated beings the force of circumstances has converted us into. We are the very embodiment of pastoral simplicity from time to time, Bickenbach and I.'

' And in what particular spot are you thinking of giving play to your pastoral dispositions ?' inquired Colborne, who could not help fancying that this announcement conveyed something in the nature of an invitation.

'Oh, not in any very remote spot. Only at Enghien, which is reached by frequent trains from the Gare du Nord, but which is rustic enough for our purpose. You ought to visit Enghien and Montmorency some fine

day, and pay the tribute of a sigh to the
memory of Jean Jacques Rousseau, if you
have ever heard of that writer. Now I must
not detain your friend's fiery horse any longer.
Tell him—your friend, I mean—that I shall
not be offended with him for passing me, if
he can.'

Douglas Colborne did not deliver the above
polite message, nor, in spite of plain and
direct queries, did Mr. Lindsay learn what
had passed between him and the Countess
Radna during their brief interview; but it
seems almost superfluous to mention that the
hero of this narrative was taking a return
ticket for Enghien shortly before mid-day on
the morrow. The railway journey to Enghien
occupies half an hour or thereabouts, and so
astute had been his calculations that he felt
able to count with tolerable certainty upon
the fact that two ladies of Continental habits
who proposed to spend a day in the country
would find it necessary to partake of a *déjeuner
à la fourchette* between twelve and one o'clock.
An Englishwoman might probably take a
packet of sandwiches with her and eat them
out of doors ; but such Spartan abstinence
was hardly to be expected of those who had

had nothing but a cup of coffee and a roll to sustain them since rising from their beds. On alighting from the train, therefore, he proceeded straight to the principal restaurant in the place, where he was rewarded by the sight of the Countess Radna and the Baroness von Bickenbach, who were seated at a little round table in the public dining-room, and one of whom, at least, did not seem to be at all more surprised by this encounter than he himself was.

'So you have come,' said she composedly, as he approached, and while the worthy Bickenbach was giving vent to sundry guttural and perfunctory exclamations of astonishment; 'I thought you would, and I shouldn't wonder if you were under the impression that I wanted you to come.'

He began to protest that he had entertained no such audacious hope; but she interrupted him by saying laughingly, 'Oh, I did want you; why not? Sit down and order some food for yourself. I have eaten as much as I want; but the appetite of our dear friend on the other side of the table knows no bounds, and you will finish before she has done even now, if you make haste.'

Bickenbach, whose accomplishments included only a very elementary knowledge of the English language, nodded encouragingly at him, and he soon found that she well deserved the reputation claimed for her by her patroness. For his own part, he had no wish to enter into competition with her, and although, to keep up appearances, he disposed of some cutlets and fried potatoes, he was far less eager to appease the pangs of hunger than to ascertain what was to be done and what he would be expected to do on the conclusion of the repast.

The Countess, who sat watching him with an amused expression of countenance from beneath her half-closed eyelids—and who, after uttering the above recorded sentences, was pleased to continue the conversation in French —relieved his mind of all anxiety upon that point by calmly issuing her commands as she rose from the table.

'Bickenbach,' said she, 'is going to sketch the lake. In the matter of sketching and painting in water-colours Bickenbach is *de première force* and ought not to have her attention distracted by the chatter of inartistic neighbours. While she is at work, you and

I will walk to Montmorency; or perhaps we will only sit down somewhere in the shade and talk. At any rate, we have the whole afternoon before us; so that it is quite unnecessary to decide at once how we will spend it.'

The programme had a seductive sound, and it was not, at all events, for him to offer any objections to the carrying out of it. After paying his modest bill, he accompanied the two ladies to the margin of the lake, whither the excellent Bickenbach's easel and camp-stool and other paraphernalia had already been transported, and when he had seen her comfortably established beneath a gigantic white umbrella he was willing enough to walk to Montmorency or any other destination with the Countess Radna, who beckoned him away, remarking, ' Now, for the next hour or two, we can do and say exactly what we please.'

It did not please her to make a pious pilgrimage to the spots rendered classic by memories of the author of ' La Nouvelle Héloise.' She said the sun was too hot for violent exercise, and confessed, besides, that she was no very enthusiastic admirer of Jean Jacques. ' Although,' she added, ' he knew

a good deal—more, perhaps, than we do, in
spite of our having, in one sense, so completely
outstripped him. All things considered, philo-
sophy is hardly worth the trouble, is it?
Nobody really knows anything, and the best
thing we can do is to plod along, with our
eyes fixed upon the ground and a firm conviction that nothing outside the range of our
short vision is of much importance to us as
individuals. That, I am sure, is your opinion.'

She seated herself, as she spoke, upon the
grass beneath a spreading chestnut-tree, and
Colborne hastened to follow her example. ' I
suppose we all know what our immediate
duties are, and I suppose the main thing is
that we should do our best to fulfil them,' was
his highly practical rejoinder.

'No doubt; and what do you regard as
your immediate duties ? It might be interesting to hear about them and how you
arrived at the point of being certain that you
can recognise them.'

He gave her the desired information with
perfect readiness and simplicity of diction. It
was incumbent upon him, he thought, to
study agriculture, with a view to rendering
his property somewhat more productive.

Without pretending to be a political sage, he claimed some acquaintance with British domestic politics, and was inclined to believe that, if a seat in Parliament could be found for him, he ought to secure it and add such personal weight as he possessed to that of the patriots who were gallantly striving to push the wheels of the State in the right direction through the mire of an obstructive Opposition. He considered, furthermore, that he owed allegiance to those principles of conduct which have from time immemorial been held to be obligatory upon Christians and gentlemen ; and he wound up (although he had not been invited to tag a moral on to his profession of faith) by observing that those who set their own amusement before themselves as their chief object in life were very unlikely, by his way of thinking, to get any amusement out of life at all.

'You say that for me,' remarked the Countess composedly. 'I don't know who told you that I lived only for my own amusement, but nothing can be more positive than that I haven't succeeded in amusing myself as yet. Still, I admit, with gratitude, that you are amusing, for the moment.'

'You mean, I suppose, that I am an ass.
All the same, I don't see why I am an ass.
You yourself admit that nobody can look
much further ahead than the length of his
nose.'

'And don't you ever look further ahead
than that ? What about those ideas of yours
respecting your home politics which brought
quite a fine colour into your cheeks when
you mentioned them ? Oh, you will go far,
and your nose will go on in front of you ;
you have only to follow it, as it will follow
your will. The difference between you and
me is that I can't follow my nose, because I
have no will to direct it. It is turning for-
lornly this way and that, sniffing the air and
detecting no symptom of scent anywhere.'

Now, it is no very difficult matter for a
man possessed of ordinary common-sense to
point out that plenty of scent, true and false,
is discoverable at all points of the compass.
The time slipped away quite pleasantly while
Colborne expounded his modest creed and
endeavoured to apply it to the case of his
companion, who, to tell the truth, was by no
means averse to discussing herself. She
affected to laugh his panaceas to scorn, but

she confessed that she was not yet an absolutely convinced pessimist, and perhaps the
conclusion at which he arrived after a prolonged interchange of ideas was not so very
far removed from being a correct one.

'The long and the short of it is,' said he,
'that what you want is somebody whom you
can care for more than you care for yourself.
And, of course, you will meet with such a
person one of these days.'

'Shall I ? That doesn't seem to me to be
proved. If he is to appear at all—naturally,
you are speaking of *him*, not of her or them—
he ought to have made his appearance by this
time, ought he not ? Since you are so confident of his existence, will you tell me what
he will be like ? It would save me trouble to
be able to recognise him at a glance.'

She was looking full at her interlocutor
from beneath her sunshade, and he was conscious that her glance gave the spur to his
heart. Nevertheless, he was also conscious—
as, indeed, he had been throughout the interview—that he would be a double-dyed fool if
he were to let himself fall in love with one
who not only was, but considered herself to be,
so far above him in rank.

'I'm sure I don't know what the happy
man will be like,' he answered, with a half-
smothered sigh, 'and I'm sure I don't want
to know. I should probably detest him if I
could see him, even with the mind's eye ; so
it's just as well that I can't.'

She raised her eyebrows.

' Why should you detest this shadowy personage ?' she inquired innocently.

' Doesn't one always detest the people who
marry one's friends ?'

' *Comme vous y allez !*—I had no idea that
I had the honour of being a friend of yours.'
But, perceiving that his feelings were rather
more wounded by this speech than she had
intended them to be, she hastened to add :
' Not that I object to being your friend ; pray
don't imagine that. On the contrary, I ask
nothing better. Let us agree to be friends,
then, if you will have it so, and let us shake
hands upon it, after the custom of your
people.'

Nothing will ever convince foreign nations
that we are not perpetually shaking hands,
nor is it possible to persuade them that we do
not habitually devour underdone beef. These
irremovable misapprehensions, with the con-

sequences thereof, must be submitted to, and, in truth, the consequences of the former are apt to be less unpleasant than those of the latter. Douglas Colborne certainly did not find it unpleasant to take the Countess's cool, white hand ; yet her fingers had not remained for more than a few seconds within his clasp when he became aware, with a sudden, sharp shock, of something that was likely to bring a great deal of unpleasantness into his future life. Not all his prudence, nor all his clear realization of the circumstances, could help him ; he knew, beyond the shadow of a doubt, that what he had scarcely gone the length of dreading was now an actual fact, and that there could never be any question of friendship between him and the Countess Radna.

And while he looked at her, sitting there in the sunshine, with a half-mocking smile upon her lips, he discerned a barely perceptible change in her expression which told him that she had read what was in his mind. Neither of them spoke for a minute or two ; he was horribly disconcerted, but she did not appear to be in the least so, and presently she rose, remarking that it was time to go and examine the results of Bickenbach's labours. So he followed her in silence to the spot where the worthy Baroness was hard at work, when she surprised him by saying composedly :

'Mr. Colborne has come to bid you adieu ; he has to return to Paris by the next train. You and I, my Bickenbach, will spend the rest of the day here and go home at nightfall, like a couple of good *bourgeoises.*'

She did not offer to shake hands with him a second time, but took leave of him with a friendly little motion of her head, and he was fain to depart. inwardly abusing himself for his clumsiness and stupidity, while acknowledging that he had, upon the whole, been mercifully dealt with.

Nevertheless, he felt, as he strode towards the railway-station, that the matter could not end there and then. Clumsy and stupid he might have been, and presumptuous into the bargain ; yet he was not quite humble enough to submit to being good-humouredly waved aside, like an importunate beggar. And if some less merciful method of dismissal was in store for him—as, no doubt, it was—it must be formulated before he could make his final bow of withdrawal and resignation.

CHAPTER IV.

A QUALIFIED CONGÉ.

It does not seem very extravagant to assume
that the majority of those who will honour
this unpretending work with their perusal are
acquainted either with the passion of love, or
with some such semblance of it as may do
duty for an equivalent ; so that they will, it
is to be hoped, readily understand Douglas
Colborne's condition of mind.   He had to tell
the Countess Radna in plain words that he
loved her.   That she would refuse him might
be a foregone conclusion ; that she would be
astonished at his impudence was not improbable.   Still, he owed it to himself and to
the sincerity of his sentiments to be defeated
before accepting a defeat.

   The above being his view of the situation,
it evidently behoved him to lose no time in

picking up the thread of their intercourse at a
point where, if he had had all his wits about
him, he would not perhaps have suffered it to
drop ; and a justly irritated man he was when
he found that, do what he would, he was
unable to carry so simple and straightforward
a programme into effect. It was not very
difficult to meet the Countess, and, as a
matter of fact, he did meet her three or four
times during the course of the ensuing week ;
but it was impossible to speak to her in
private without her consent, and this she was
apparently determined to withhold from him.
Through the kindly intervention of Lady
Royston, he obtained admission to various
entertainments where the Countess Radna
shone resplendent ; he was permitted to join
the throng which surrounded her, and to bask
for a few minutes at a time in her smiles, but
she did not let him draw her away from the
throng, nor would she let him into her house.
He called upon her twice, but was turned
back from the door both times, and really had
not the face to make a third attempt. She
would see him, no doubt, on her reception-
day ; but what would be the use of that ?

 Meanwhile, he had already exceeded what

he had mentally decided upon as the term of
his visit to the French capital ; he must soon
return home. He understood, or thought that
he understood, that the woman whom he loved
was merely anxious to spare him and herself
a more or less painful scene, and he could not
but admit that her behaviour was both reasonable and considerate. All the same, that
painful scene must needs take place. He
would never be able to forgive himself if he
were to shirk it ; and he was debating in
complete perplexity by what means it was to
be brought about, when, wandering down
the Faubourg Saint-Honoré one afternoon, he
encountered a little old lady who was holding
up her petticoats in both hands, thus display-
ing a pair of thick ankles and immense flat-
soled feet to the gaze of the irreverent. He
placed himself unhesitatingly in her path, and,
removing his hat, said :

' How do you do, Madame von Bickenbach ?
May I have a word with you ?'

The little old lady dropped her skirts in
order to throw up her hands. Perhaps she
was really not so much surprised as she
always appeared to be when anybody accosted
her ; but the habit of affecting this amiable

astonishment had become a second nature
to her.

'*Ach, Herr Je!*' she exclaimed in her native
tongue ; 'how you startled me!'

Douglas Colborne, who did not speak
German, proceeded to explain himself in his
best French. He wanted, he said, without
circumlocution, to know why the Countess
Radna refused to receive him. Also, whether
there was any particular day or hour when he
might count upon finding her at home and
disengaged. He would be leaving for England
shortly, and he had reasons for wishing to
speak to the Countess alone, before he started
on his journey. This statement, of course,
was compromisingly explicit, but he desired
to be explicit, and was quite willing to com-
promise himself.

Bickenbach made a series of extraordinary
grimaces, which, if he had only known it
(but, indeed, they hardly spoke for themselves), were designed to express sentimental
sympathy.

'*Mon bon monsieur,*' said she (her actual
words were '*Mon pon mossié*'), 'you can
have nothing to tell the Countess that she
does not already know. There have been so

many like you ! It is a pity ; but there is no
help for it, and if you will take the advice of
an old woman that wishes you nothing but
good, you will rest satisfied with having
made her cry. *Ma parole d'honneur !* she
cried, after we had returned from Enghien
the other day—which, for the rest, proves
very little. Go home, dear sir, and forget us.
We ourselves are about to quit Paris, for we
always visit our estates in Hungary at this
time of year.'

'You will not, if I can help it, leave before
I have seen you—that is, before I have seen
the Countess Radna,' Colborne declared.
'What you say is kindly meant, I am sure ;
but, as I dare say you will understand, it
comes too late to be of any service to me.
You might do me a genuine service by
begging the Countess to grant me a farewell
interview.'

Bickenbach shrugged up her shoulders.

'As you please,' she replied. 'I cannot
tell whether the Countess will receive you or
not, but probably she will, and probably you
will wish afterwards that she had not. The
Countess has a heart of gold, yet she often
causes great suffering to others, because she

has difficulty in believing that they are sincere. *Enfin!* since it is your wish——'

It was most decidedly his wish and his determination to take personal leave of this sceptical lady, whose scepticism, he flattered himself, was unlikely to remain proof against the declaration which he had to make to her. He was curious to know in what fashion she would give him his *congé*, that was all —that, and a pardonable disinclination to retreat until he should be compelled to do so. Therefore he thanked the friendly Baroness, saying that he counted upon her to deliver his message, which she promised to do.

'Only,' said she, on parting with him, 'you are asking for something which cannot make you happy, and may make you very unhappy. Pray remember afterwards that I warned you of that. You will see that she will treat you as she has treated the others.'

Douglas Colborne did not quite like this repeated allusion to 'the others'; still, of course there must have been others—heaps of others—and, after all, what difference did it make to him? At least, she had not apparently lost her heart to any of the others. So, all things considered, he was disposed to be grateful to his lucky star for having caused him to run against the Baroness von Bickenbach, and his satisfaction was complete when the post of the following morning brought him a short note, written in a large straggling hand upon very thick paper, which was embellished by an enormous coronet and monogram. The note, notwithstanding its brevity, was all that he could have wished or expected it to be :

'DEAR MR. COLBORNE,

    'I hear from my excellent Bickenbach that you are anxious to make your adieux to me before leaving the country. That is most amiable of you, and if you will look in between five and six o'clock to-morrow evening, you will find me at home, and enchanted to profit by this occasion of wishing you *bon voyage*.

        'H. R.'

Well, the words, when they had been read over a dozen times, did, no doubt, seem to have a certain ironical ring ; but what of that ? She would have been fairly entitled to laugh at him for having fallen in love with her after so brief an acquaintanceship, even if she had not been the Countess Radna and the proprietress of vast estates. So when he reached her house at the hour which she had specified, and, after giving his name, was admitted to an audience, he had nothing but the most deferential gratitude to express for the favour accorded to him. The day had been a hot one, and the room in which she received him was still darkened by closed *persiennes*. Entering it from the bright outer light, he could scarcely distinguish her features, and was but vaguely aware of the exquisite salmon-coloured tea-gown, the pink ribbons, and the old Mechlin lace which formed her costume.

'That is all very well,' said she; 'but, notwithstanding your pretty speeches, I am under no illusion as to the motive which has procured me the honour of this visit. To come to the point at once, you are here for the purpose of quarrelling with me—isn't it so?'

Douglas Colborne protested that nothing could be more remote from his intentions. Why should he wish to quarrel with her? And why in the world should she impute so improbable a desire to him?

'Would it be so very improbable? I treated you like an intimate friend only a short time ago ; I have taken some trouble to hold you at arm's length ever since. It would have been perfectly excusable on your part to stop my duenna in the street and demand an interview with me and an explanation, to which I should have made you welcome. Am I to understand that all you demanded was an interview ? And, if so, why did you demand it ?'

'Merely because I was resolved to tell you in so many words what you know without being told,' he replied. 'It is just because you know it, and because I know you know it, that an explanation would be superfluous. You may say that a declaration from me is equally superfluous, and so perhaps it is ; yet I must make it, notwithstanding its superfluity. Of course it is quite absurd of me to love you, of course you can only give me one answer, and of course it has been kind of you to do what you could to spare me the mortification of being laughed at. But I really don't think that I so very much mind your laughing at me. What I should have minded a great deal more would have been the feeling of having slunk off home without having been absolutely and distinctly rejected.'

'Oh, if absolute and distinct rejection will
satisfy you,' said the Countess, 'you are not
hard to please, and what you wish for is quite
at your service. As for my laughing at you,
that is another matter. Certainly I do not
mean to marry you ; but I cannot see anything so irresistibly comic in the idea of your
having fallen in love with me.'

'No ; there is nothing comic or extraordinary in that,' he agreed, with a sigh.
'What I meant was that your immense
superiority to me in respect of rank and
wealth——'

'Ah, bah !' she interrupted ; 'in your
world and mine gradations of rank count for
very little, and superiority of wealth only
counts, or ought only to count, amongst our
inferiors. I will not pay you so poor a compliment as to assume that you prostrate yourself before me—it is an unbecoming attitude,
Mr. Colborne—simply because my family is
an old one, and because I own more leagues
of grazing land and vineyards than I have ever
cared to reckon up.'

'These are genuine obstacles,' he returned,
'and I dare say you would acknowledge them
to be so, if you didn't feel that there was

another obstacle so great as to make them
sink into insignificance. You don't love me,
and you never could love me; that, to be sure,
is reason enough, without troubling to mention
the rest.'

'Well, I am afraid it is. Still, there are
other obstacles which might be mentioned, and
which are of greater force than those that you
call genuine. Husband and wife ought to be
of the same religion; and I am even more
profoundly separated from you than I should
be if I were a devout Roman Catholic, for I
have no religion at all. Husband and wife
ought to have the same interests; and I do
not think that I could possibly interest myself
in the things which interest you. Finally, a
husband ought to be his wife's master, and I
have not the habit of obedience. Go home to
your mother and your sisters and your
English life, dear Mr. Colborne, and congratulate yourself upon the circumstance that,
since you had to fall in love for a few days
with somebody, you have chanced upon a
woman who, notwithstanding all her faults, is
not cruel enough to embitter the remainder of
your existence for you.'

'I don't think I quite understand you,' said

the young man, with a puzzled frown ; 'perhaps you don't quite understand me, either. If it is true, as you say it is, that you have no religion, I am very sorry ; but that doesn't prevent me from loving you, nor do I believe that your tastes are really so unlike mine as to make the difference worth considering, supposing that you could care for me. After all, the question begins and ends there, doesn't it ? You make light of the difficulties which are very obvious to me, and I can't see much cogency in those that you speak of; we both know that if the one supreme difficulty could be surmounted, we should snap our fingers at the rest. Believe, at least, that I love you, and that I always shall love you. I don't think it is asking too much of you to ask that.'

He spoke with a certain concentrated vehemence which was not without visible effect upon the composure of his companion. However, she recovered herself without any great effort, and observed laughingly :

'Very few people think it unreasonable to ask for a miracle ; millions ask for miracles every day, in the most matter-of-fact way, when they say their prayers. If, by a miracle,

I should ever take to saying mine again, I
shall not forget to request that this infatuation
of yours may be shortened by a slight interference with the ordinary course of nature. In
a word, Mr. Colborne, I do not love you ; so
I presume there is nothing more to be said,
except good-bye.'

She rose and held out her hand, which he
made so bold as to raise to his lips. There
was nothing more to be said, and he moved
towards the door without another word. But
upon the threshold he was arrested by the
sound of her voice.

'By the way,' said she, as coolly as if he
had been a mere every-day visitor, 'were
you ever at Bagnères de Luchon, in the
Pyrenees ?'

He had never heard of that watering-place,
and he confessed as much, with a surprised
and inquiring look.

'I thought it was just possible that your
wanderings might have taken you there,
because all young Englishmen, when they
wander, make for the mountains. I asked
because Bickenbach and I think of taking up
our quarters at Luchon in the month of
August.'

'You will find me there when you arrive,' Colborne declared, a sudden rush of hope causing his heart to leap up.

'Indeed ? Well, that would not be an actual miracle ; although I confess that I shall be profoundly astonished if you keep your promise. In any case, you have given me an excuse to substitute *au revoir* for the ugly word *adieu.*'

Thereupon she retired through a door facing that of which he held the handle between his fingers, and he left the house a happier and more sanguine man than he had been on entering it.

CHAPTER V.

IF Douglas Colborne had known a little more than he did about the woman whom he loved, he would probably have been less elated than he was by her parting words. Dr. Schott could have told him, and Bickenbach could have told him (only she would not have done so), that the Countess Radna never willingly parted with an admirer, that she was quite as greedy of admiration as the rest of her sex, and that, although the kindness of her own heart would not permit her to deliberately break the heart of a fellow-creature, experience had rendered her absolutely sceptical as to the fragility of that organ. They might have added that she had taken a fancy to the young Englishman, that psychological studies always possessed a certain fascination for her, and that Luchon is not quite the liveliest place in Europe. But of course he knew no more about her than that he loved her with all his heart and soul—which seemed to be enough.

He was a simple-minded fellow (which really is not the same thing as being a fool, though nine people out of ten think that it is), and his simplicity very often led him to conclusions which, for wisdom and accuracy, were equal to any that Solomon himself could have formulated. Since, for his weal or woe, he loved this Hungarian Countess as it is only given to mortals to love once during their sojourn here below, and since she had plainly invited him to join her in the South before the end of the summer, one thing at least was evident, whatever else might be doubtful, namely, that he must so frame his plans as to respond to her invitation. A good many other things were, of course, doubtful; but it was better that some of them should be so than that they should have been placed beyond doubt in the sense which he had anticipated before his visit to the Avenue Friedland; while, as for the remainder—well, they were hardly ripe for consideration yet.

Thus he mused as he made his way towards the hotel where he was staying ; and certain further cogitations and vain imaginings, upon which it is needless to dwell, had made him quite cheerful by the time that he reached his destination, where a letter from his mother was awaiting him. Mrs. Colborne wrote such a vast number of letters every day that it would have been a matter of physical impossibility for her to make any of them lengthy : on the other hand, her missives were usually to the point and invariably pleasant. This one was quite pleasant as regarded diction, notwithstanding its somewhat reproving tone. The writer gave her son to understand that he had dallied long enough in Capua, and ought now to return without delay to the special duties and pleasures assigned to him by Heaven. 'Besides,' was her last sentence, 'I have something important to tell you about ; so please telegraph to say by what train you will arrive.'

Mrs. Colborne received her telegram and, not many hours after it had been delivered to her, had the additional pleasure of receiving

her son. He was a very obedient and satisfactory sort of son, as sons go, and she had
never had any reason to be seriously displeased with him. Nor, for the matter of
that, had he ever had reason to be seriously
displeased with her, although she and he were
not altogether in sympathy with each other.

Everybody who has had the opportunity of
doing so must have noticed the sympathy
between mothers and sons which is so common
as to be almost universal in France and so
rare as to be almost phenomenal in our own
country. Perhaps we are a more independent
race than our neighbours across the Channel,
and perhaps independence may have its drawbacks as well as its advantages. In any case,
the very last thing that Douglas Colborne
would have thought of doing would have
been to confide to his mother the fact that he
had fallen desperately in love with a foreign
Countess. He had nothing so startling as
that to say to her when he reached Stoke
Leighton, the pleasant and desirable-looking
estate, situated on the borders of Berkshire
and Buckinghamshire, which now owned him
as its sole lord. There had been Colbornes at
Stoke Leighton for many generations, and if

the Colbornes of years gone by had been
wealthier people than their present representative, the fault did not lie with him. Free
trade was to blame for the change; the ex-
travagance of some ancestors and the careless-
ness of others were also to blame; but it was
not Douglas Colborne's habit to blame anybody,
and the sight of the old red-brick house which
he loved aroused no other feelings in his heart
than those which the sight of home ought
always to arouse in the breasts of honest
folks. He was not rich; but, then, he did not
particularly covet riches, hoping only that,
by dint of thrift and management, he might
be able to live in accordance with hereditary
traditions. To accomplish that much was,
from a pecuniary point of view, the summit of
his ambition.

Mrs. Colborne may possibly and excusably
have aspired to something a little more pre-
tentious than that on his behalf. In fact, she
hastened to assure him that she did, after she
had poured out a cup of tea for him in her
boudoir, and had listened complacently to his
declared conviction that there was no country
like England after all.

'There is no harm in seeing other countries

and other people,' said she, with a fine toleration, 'and I hope you will continue to make
excursions abroad every now and then, like
the rest of the world. But, of course, your
chief interest will have to be in your career;
and what with cricket and hunting and
shooting, and the terrible length to which
Parliamentary sessions run in these days, I
am afraid you will never be able to absent
yourself for more than a week or two at a
time.'

Mrs. Colborne was a small, alert woman,
who had once been pretty and was still quite
nice-looking, in spite of her gray hair. She
had charming manners, she was universally
popular; she had a keen, if somewhat restricted, sense of duty, and it had been her
consistent endeavour to deserve the reputation
which she enjoyed as the best of wives and
mothers. Her late husband, a heavy, inert
personage, had sometimes complained feebly
of her superabundant energy, but nobody
had ever thought of attaching importance to
the complaints of the late Mr. Colborne. It
was generally and very justly recognised that
nothing except his wife's energy had preserved
him from drifting into bankruptcy.

'Oh, the Parliamentary sessions, eh?' said her son, smiling. 'Does that mean that I am to be pitchforked into Parliament?'

'Well, I hope so : it was on account of that that I telegraphed to you. Poor old Mr. Majendie has had another bad attack of gout, and has at last announced that he doesn't intend to seek re-election. So, you see, it is really important that you should be upon the spot and ready to come forward.'

'As a Tory, I presume?'

'Naturally. You don't propose to come forward as a Radical, do you?'

'No ; only I am not sure that I am quite such a fossil as to be a worthy successor to old Majendie. However, I dare say a majority of the electors may have realized that the nineteenth century is nearly at an end, and may vote for me rather than for a Gladstonian, even though they may not share all my opinions. I shall have to communicate with the people at headquarters before I venture to recommend myself to this enlightened con-stituency, though, shan't I?'

'Oh, that has been done already. Peggy Rowley has espoused your cause, and she, as you know, is a host in herself. It is lucky

for you that you have such an influential supporter at your back.'

'I am very much indebted to her, I'm sure,'
answered Douglas, in a tone which to a sensitive ear might have conveyed the impression
that he did not so very much enjoy being
indebted to anybody. As a matter of fact,
the sincere attachment which he felt for his
friend and neighbour Miss Rowley did not
prevent him from wishing that she would
kindly permit him to manage his own affairs
in his own way. But it would have been ungracious to say this, and he was aware that
he would hurt his mother's feelings if he did
say it; so he changed the subject.

'Are the girls all right?' he asked. 'What
has become of them?'

'They are all right,' answered Mrs. Colborne. 'They have gone out in the pony-cart,
I believe. I dare say they will be in presently.'

Presently they came in—fat, good-humoured
Loo, who was older than her brother, and
who had accepted in advance the *rôle* of an
old maid, which her homely features rather
than her years appeared to have allotted to
her; followed by Phyllis, a tall, dark, hand-

some girl, whose resolute little mouth, per-
fectly-fitting costume, and air of conscious
superiority to her elder sister, seemed to indi-
cate that she had realized the responsibilities
which devolved upon her as the beauty of the
family. They were both of them affectionate
in their welcome, and eager to hear what
special attractions had caused Douglas to pro-
long his stay in Paris. Their curiosity, it is
needless to say, was not gratified ; nor was it
participated in by Mrs. Colborne, who was an
optimist, and who, having made up her mind
that her son was eventually to espouse Miss
Rowley, could not imagine that he would be
provoking enough to think of marrying anybody else. While the girls were drinking
their tea, and expressing their high appreciation of the presents of jewellery which their
brother had not forgotten to purchase for
them, she was preoccupied with her own little
ideas, and, after the manner of parents, paid
but slight attention to the chatter of her
offspring ; but at length she broke silence to
remark :

' There is a garden-party at Swinford to-
morrow. Of course you will come, and then
Peggy will tell you all about it. She under-

stands these things a great deal better than I do.'

Douglas sighed.

'I do so hate garden-parties!' said he. 'Couldn't I find some other and more comfortable opportunity of seeing Peg and hearing all about it? There is plenty of time, you know; we aren't upon the eve of a General Election yet.'

'We may be upon the eve of Mr. Majendie's death, though,' observed his mother. 'One hopes that the poor old man may live for a great many years to come, but gout in the stomach is a very serious thing. I really don't think you can afford to be idle.'

'You ought to be there, Douglas,' said Phyllis decisively. 'She knows that you were to come home to-day, and, after all the trouble that she has taken for you, the least you can do is to accept her invitation.'

'Besides,' chimed in Loo, 'she will be so awfully disappointed if you don't turn up.'

'Far be it from me,' said Douglas, 'to inflict an undeserved disappointment upon my benefactress. I suppose she is my benefactress, and I suppose it is my duty to thank her, isn't it?'

Both the young ladies opined that it was,
while Mrs. Colborne remarked for the second
time that he was lucky in possessing so ener-
getic and capable a partisan. Perhaps Mrs.
Colborne was right, and undoubtedly he would
owe a debt of gratitude to Peggy Rowley if
she should manage to secure a seat in Parliament for him, because he was really more
anxious to get into the House of Commons
than to achieve any other success, save and
except that impossible one of winning the
Countess Radna's heart; still, he not unnaturally felt that he would prefer, for choice,
to win an election upon his own merits, such
as they were. However, he accompanied his
mother and sisters to the garden-party at
Swinford Manor on the following afternoon,
and received that warm welcome from the
lady of the manor which past experience had
justified him in anticipating.

Miss Margaret Rowley was by no means so
wealthy and magnificent a lady as the Countess
Radna, but she occupied a position quite as
independent, and enjoyed an income more
than sufficient for her personal needs. Like
the Countess, she was an only child and an
orphan; like her, she was sole mistress of

many acres of land ; but, unlike her, she
was not in the least discontented with her
lot. If everybody liked Peggy Rowley, that
was doubtless because Peggy Rowley liked
everybody—or almost everybody. She had
aristocratic connections and an enormous
acquaintance ; her father had been a politician
who had held high offices, and after his death
she had not lost sight of her friends ; the
world had never given her cause to quarrel
with it, nor had she ever dreamt of doing so
on account of its many imperfections—which,
to be sure, were less apparent to her than
they were to the lady who had fascinated her
old playmate, Douglas Colborne. She was
a year older than her former playmate ; she
was probably justified in deeming herself
somewhat wiser and more experienced ; she
had certainly seen far more of society, political
and other, than he had, and had been free to
follow her own bent for a much longer period.
Considering how young she still was, she
possessed quite an extraordinary amount of
political and social influence, counting Cabinet
Ministers amongst her intimates, and associa-
ting habitually with those great ladies who
may not be as absolutely great in these days

as they used to be, yet continue to be a power in the land. Where the Countess unquestionably had the advantage over her was in point of comeliness ; for it must be confessed that Peggy Rowley was no beauty. At the same time, she was not plain : she had to some extent the *beauté du diable*. If her features were irregular, and if her colouring was of that indeterminate brown shade which gave the very few people who wished to depreciate her an excuse for describing her as whitey-brown, she had white teeth, the clear complexion of health, and a neat little figure : for an heiress, she was anything but bad-looking, and it was only by her own good-will and pleasure that she remained a spinster.

'So here you are, back from your travels,' said she, as Douglas Colborne crossed the lawn, which was crowded with her guests, to shake hands with her. 'How did you like the Roystons? And how did you like Paris? Come and see my gloxinias and tell me all about it.'

He followed her towards the hot-house, which she indicated by a wave of her sunshade, but did not immediately comply with her other request.

'Isn't it you who are going to tell me all about it?' he asked. 'I thought it was; or, at all events, that was what my mother thought and gave me to understand. In fact, she mentioned your being able to tell me all about it as an overwhelming inducement to me to attend a garden-party.'

'You haven't stayed long enough in France to get rid of your insular candour, I see. Never mind, I can forgive you. Garden-parties *are* a bore, I admit, and I shouldn't give them if I could help it; but I am glad you have overcome your repugnance to them for once, because, of course, we must talk over this election business. It will be all right, I hope. Everybody wants you to come forward, including old Mr. Majendie, who is here to-day, by-the-bye, and who wants to speak to you. You won't have a walk over; but I haven't the slightest doubt you will win, unless something utterly unforeseen occurs between this and then. Only we must begin to bestir ourselves, you know; it won't do to let things slide until the last moment.'

She gave him a rapid and concise account of the measures which she had already taken on his behalf. Apparently nothing more was required of him than to make a considerable number of speeches and to abstain, if possible, from making a conspicuous fool of himself. It was all very well, and he could only express his sincere thanks to her and to those who had acted with her ; yet it did strike him that he had been treated rather like a lay figure, and that his individual opinions, wishes, and convictions had not been held worthy of being taken into account.

'And what if I were to kick over the traces ?' he inquired at length, half laughingly.

'Oh, you won't do that. In fact, I don't see how you can ; because the old Tory party is extinct, and has left no traces behind it to be kicked over. However advanced you may be, there is no fear of your being more advanced than your constituents. Only you must be able to say " shibboleth " without lisping, which I should think would be within the range of your powers. You haven't deigned to glance at my poor gloxinias yet. Aren't they glorious ?'

They were far more glorious than the prospects of Toryism in this country, and he paid them the tribute of admiration that they

deserved ; but his hostess had no admiration
to spare for the Democratic Conservative
principles which he proceeded to expound,
nor did she seem to think that his principles
were of any great consequence.

'The main thing is to win the election,'
said she. 'When once you have done that it
will be your business to reconcile your ideas
with those of your chief, or to make him
reconcile his with yours, if you are strong
enough. Now, let us hear what you did with
yourself in Paris, besides dining at the
Embassy and seeing the Grand Prix run.'

She very soon found out from him as much
as she wanted to know. He did not absolutely admit her into his confidence ; but she
was so old and so true a friend that he had
no hesitation in mentioning the Countess
Radna to her (he had not mentioned the
Countess Radna to his mother), and she drew
her own conclusions from his artless description of that lady. Whether those conclusions
were satisfactory to her or not nobody could
have divined from her face, which betrayed
no emotion beyond a kindly and sympathetic
interest ; but at the end of a quarter of an
hour she cut short his remarks by declaring

that she had neglected her guests long enough and reminding him that he ought not to leave without saying a few words to Mr. Majendie.

Mr. Majendie, a frail old gentleman, whose withered cheeks were as white as his beard, and who had been an intimate friend of the late Mr. Colborne, held out his hand to his probable successor with many amiable professions of good-will.

' I have fought my fight,' said he (not that he had ever fought with much ferocity) ; ' now the time has come for me to be helped out of the lists and for a younger man to put on the armour which has become too heavy for me to wear. I couldn't wish it to be donned by a more promising aspirant than your father's son.'

He then gave utterance to the customary commonplaces, and intimated that such powers as he still possessed would be very much at the service of the new candidate. ' However,' he added with a smile, ' Miss Rowley can do a great deal more for you than I can. She means to get you in, and it is written that Miss Rowley shall always have her own way.'

That might be so ; but perhaps it was not

written that Douglas Colborne should always have his own way, nor even that Mrs. Colborne should always have hers.

'What have you done to affront Peggy Rowley?' the latter inquired of her son, as they set off on their homeward drive. 'She told me just now that you were not half as wise and sober as you looked, and that I should find that out some fine day. I wonder what she meant.'

'I can't think,' answered Douglas, who, however, was not without some suspicion of Miss Rowley's meaning.

'Well,' observed Mrs. Colborne more cheerfully, after a pause, 'at all events you have a fair prospect of getting into Parliament now; and, if you do get in, you will owe your success chiefly to her. I hope you won't forget that.'

'I am sure you will never allow me to do so,' returned her son rather dryly.

CHAPTER VI.

Miss Rowley was far too prominent a figure in contemporary society, and far too much enamoured of the part which she played as a member of it, to linger for more than a day or two in her country residence at that early period of the summer. She had a little town house in Mayfair to which she betook herself soon after her garden-party, accompanied by old Miss Spofforth, her duenna ; so that Douglas Colborne had no immediate opportunity of asking her why she had been so inconsiderate as to express doubts respecting his wisdom and sobriety to his mother. But, as has been said, he was able to conjecture, without need for positive information, what she had had in her mind when she had been guilty of that indiscretion, and the only effect it had upon him was to make him resolve that he himself would be less indiscreet for the future. Although he suspected that his mother wanted him to marry Peggy Rowley, he was perfectly sure that Peggy Rowley had no notion of marrying him, and he would as soon have chosen that trustworthy ally of his for a confidant as another had he felt any craving for a confidant ; but, all things considered, it seemed best to keep his own counsel and kill time somehow or other until the month of August, 'when,' thought he, 'I shall know, once for all, whether there is a shadow of a hope for me or not.'

The filling up of his time during that period of suspense was a task which presented no difficulty. From the moment that he signified his willingness to be placed in nomination by the Conservatives of the constituency as their representative at the next General Election, he found that his presence on many platforms was more or less obligatory. In addition to this, the management of the Stoke Leighton property, which he had taken into his own hands, and which for a long time past had been conducted upon very slack and un-

businesslike principles, gave him more than
a sufficiency of daily work to get through.
Even if he had had no work to do, he would
have been pretty well provided with various
forms of play ; for he was an ardent cricketer,
it had always been his custom to attend the
race-meetings and the athletic contests which
were frequented by his friends, and, as he was
a popular young man, he was reminded every
morning by a shoal of invitations that the
London season was now in full swing. He
would not have objected to taking his mother
and sisters up to town for six weeks or so ;
but Mrs. Colborne represented to him that,
both on financial and social grounds, this
would be an undesirable move. She was in
too deep mourning to go out yet ; she doubted
whether in any case she could afford to entertain, and she did not wish him to spend his
money on her. The girls might perhaps run
up for a day or two at a time to Peggy
Rowley or some other friend, but they were
quite resigned to the prospect of spending
that summer quietly at home.

‘ By next summer,’ added Mrs. Colborne
with a smile which was half regretful, half
anticipatory, ‘ the dear old place may not be

our home any longer—who knows? I shall
be very willing to leave it as soon as you
have chosen my successor, because I am sure
your choice will be a good one.'

Douglas laughed, and observed that his
choice might possibly not be that of the
person chosen ; whereupon Mrs. Colborne,
laughing also, returned confidently, ' Oh, I
think it will. But we shall see.'

Now, although the young aspirant for
Parliamentary honours felt in duty bound to
decline most of the above-mentioned invitations, he did contrive, by means of frequent
railway journeys, to put in an appearance at a
fair number of London entertainments ; and
at one of these it was at once his privilege
and his pleasure to encounter Lady Royston.
She recognised him immediately, and fore-
stalled a question which he would not have
been able to resist asking by beginning to
talk about the Countess Radna.

' Your Hungarian friend has been causing
a sensation in Vienna, I hear,' said she. ' I
suppose she rather likes producing sensations,
doesn't she ?'

' I really don't know,' answered Douglas ;
' but I shouldn't think she did: that sort of

achievement would be too easily accomplished
to excite her ambition. How has she been
scandalizing Vienna ?'

'Only by engaging herself to Count Siedenberg and breaking off her engagement at the
last moment, without any ostensible reason.
Count Siedenberg, I must tell you, is a most
magnificent personage, and the match would
have been a grand one, even for her ; but she
has chosen to throw him over, and it seems
that she has got into great disgrace at Court
about it. She pretends not to care, they say;
but of course she must care, and of course
everybody declares now that she has formed
some unfortunate attachment. I trust that
you are not the culprit.'

Lady Royston was only joking ; but the
young man's heightened colour caused her to
open her eyes and wonder whether she might
not perchance have spoken a true word in
jest ; while Peggy Rowley, who joined the
pair at this moment and who had caught her
last sentence, asked:

'What are you accusing him of? Judging
by his face, he is guilty. Now, Lady Royston, if you have been corrupting an innocent
English squire by introducing him to French

ladies of uncertain reputation, I will never
forgive you.'

Lady Royston was a good deal in awe of
Peggy Rowley, whose plain speech and abrupt
manner always affected her with a sensation
of nervous dread as to what might be coming
next. She hastened to explain that the lady
whom they had been discussing was Hungarian, not French; that her reputation was
absolutely unblemished, and that an English
squire had as little to fear from her as she had
from him.

'Oh, there *is* a lady in the case, then,' said
the relentless Peggy; 'I thought he couldn't
be blushing in that undisguised way for anything less. The same lady, perhaps,' she
added, turning to Douglas, 'about whom you
told me—the one who has everything that
the heart of woman can desire, except a
husband. And, after all, that is a blessing
which isn't desired by the heart of every
woman in the world. I forget what you said
her name was.'

Miss Rowley was speedily informed of the
lady's name, and also of the circumstance that
she had recently proved herself to be one of
those exceptional women who do not desire

to be provided with a husband. She was likewise told of the conspicuous favours which it had pleased the Countess Radna to bestow upon Douglas Colborne, and she did not fail to chaff her young friend unmercifully about his conquest. Douglas took her chaff with perfect good-humour, though he inwardly congratulated himself upon having resisted the inclination which he had felt at the time to let her into the secret. First and last, he had let Peggy into a good many of his secrets, and he had always found her friendly and sympathetic; but it was evident that she would not have sympathized with his present predicament, nor, in truth, could he have expected her to do so. She was too sensible —possibly also a little too hard—to sympathize with what was obviously ridiculous. Ridiculous it must obviously be for him to flatter himself that he had had the remotest connection with the Countess's rupture of a suitable alliance—why, indeed, should she have thought of forming such an alliance, unless she had been wholly fancy-free? Yet the fact remains that he was excited, and in some measure elated, by the news which he had heard. At the bottom of his heart he cherished a conviction that he had not been invited to travel all the way to Bagnères de Luchon for nothing. Likewise he esteemed the woman whom he loved too highly to believe that she could have been actuated by a mere ignoble wish to retain one obscure name upon the lengthy list of her admirers.

However that might be, he fully intended to keep his tryst, and was fully determined to say nothing about that intention until the time should be at hand for executing it. During the remainder of the season he met Miss Rowley pretty frequently, and they had divers long confabulations together upon political topics ; but she did not again refer to the Countess Radna, nor did he care again to introduce that lady's name into their colloquies. Early in July she left London, and it was not until the last days of that month that Mrs. Colborne's heart was gladdened by the intelligence of the impending return of her fair neighbour to Swinford Manor.

' Peggy is coming home in a week or ten days,' the unsuspecting lady announced joyfully to her son one morning. ' Now we may hope to keep you at home, too. I was afraid

you were getting bored here and that you
would be wanting to be off to Scotland or
somewhere.'

' Well, the fact is,' answered Douglas, ' that
I shall be off in a day or two. I am sorry to
miss Peggy ; but I dare say I shall find her
here when I come back. I am thinking of
spending a few weeks in the Pyrenees.'

' The Pyrenees !' echoed Mrs. Colborne,
with a look of consternation ; ' what on earth
can be taking you there ? What does one do
in the Pyrenees ? Are you going alone ?'

' Oh yes; I am going alone. I can't tell
you exactly what one does there. One shoots
isards, I believe, if one wants to shoot them,
and I suppose one ascends mountains and
admires the scenery. Anyhow, it will be a
change.'

Mrs. Colborne said all that she could in
opposition to a project which seemed to her
to be singularly ill-timed. She expressed
surprise that his engagements should permit
of his leaving England ; she represented that
he ought really to be within reach, in case of
anything happening to poor Mr. Majendie,
and she urged that even a temporary separation between him and those who were likely

to influence his election was to be deprecated ; but he had answers ready for all these objections, and she knew better than to jeopardize her power over her son by a fruitless assertion of domestic tyranny. Happily, it did not occur to her, after ascertaining that he was to travel alone, to inquire whether he expected to meet anybody on reaching his destination ; for he was a truthful man, and, had she put such a question, he would have had to give her a truthful reply.

As it was, he was not called upon to face any embarrassing examination. Phyllis, it is true, appeared to smell a rat, and displayed an inquisitive spirit which, in his capacity of her elder brother, he deemed it incumbent upon him to rebuke ; but he dealt more leniently with Loo, who only sighed and remarked :

'It is a great pity, your going away just when Peggy is expected home. I'm afraid she will think you don't care about seeing her.'

'If she thinks that,' he returned, ' she will be much mistaken. Tell her from me that, unless something altogether unforeseen happens, I shall be back in time to shoot her pheasants—not to speak of her partridges.

Between you and me, though, my dear old
Loo, I doubt whether she would break her
heart if I never came back at all.'

Loo was of a contrary opinion, and proclaimed it so emphatically as to provoke an
outburst of laughter on his part. Loo was
like his mother; she believed the ugly duck-
ling of the family to be a fit mate for any
swan, and would have been honestly amazed
at his rejection by the greatest heiress in
England. Naturally, he himself was subject
to no such illusion, nor did he for a moment
suppose that Peggy Rowley would accept his
hand and heart if he were to offer her those
treasures—which thing he had not the slightest
intention of doing. Only he did think that
Peggy was capable of making some sarcastic
remarks respecting his sudden anxiety to
inspect the Spanish frontier ; and that was
why he was not sorry to escape from the
country without bidding her farewell.

It was on the third of August that he
reached the little Pyrenean watering-place
which has always been a favourite resort of
fashionable Parisians, and has become more so
since the patriotic pride of these ladies and
gentlemen has forbidden them to disport

themselves at Baden-Baden. Luchon, lying
in a narrow green valley, hemmed in on either
side by wooded hills, above which a glimpse
of snow-clad summits may occasionally be
caught, is one of the most charming spots in
a charming region. Its loveliness is not,
perhaps, enhanced by the presence of the said
ladies and gentlemen, who, when they are not
gambling at the casino or listening to the
band, are for the most part galloping full-tilt
along the highroad on hired horses and
cracking their whips ; yet there is compensation in all things, and its hotels would doubtless be less numerous and less comfortable
without the distinguished patronage which
the place enjoys. Douglas Colborne, at all
events, had not undertaken that long, hot and
dusty journey in search of solitude ; so that
his appreciation of a good dinner on his
arrival was not marred by any sense of incon-
gruity between the chattering, gaily-attired
throng around him and the solemn, silent
mountains by which he and they were over-
shadowed. He had ascertained, by an examination of the visitors' book, that the Countess
Radna was not staying at the hotel where he
had taken up his quarters ; but this was

scarcely a disappointment to him. She had only said that she proposed to be at Luchon in the month of August; she had not specified a date, and he was quite prepared to await her advent patiently for a week or more, if need be.

His patience, as it turned out, was not subjected even to that moderate strain; for, wandering away from the hotel on the following morning, in obedience to the natural impulse which prompts those who are at the bottom of a valley to make for the top of some hill or other, he found himself all of a sudden in the presence of the lady with whom he was at the moment rehearsing an imaginary encounter. She was descending and he was ascending one of the zigzag paths which lead through the woods behind the *Établissement* to the grassy heights of Superbagnères. She was unaccompanied; she held a large bunch of wild-flowers in one hand and a long stick in the other—which was, perhaps, a sufficient reason for her accosting him merely with a bow. She was not in the least taken aback, although he, who had anticipated a meeting which must have seemed to her highly improbable, was quite deprived of the power of speech by so abrupt a fulfilment of his hopes.

'You look astonished,' she remarked, with a smile. 'Nevertheless, I understood you to say, when we parted, that I should find you here about this time.'

'Yes,' answered Douglas. recovering himself, 'and, unless I am mistaken, you answered that you would be profoundly astonished if you did.'

'Did I? I am sorry I cannot keep my word ; but it is a fact that I am not at all astonished. However. I am sincerely pleased, if that will do as well. Have you been here long ?'

He hardly knew what to make of this matter-of-course reception. He was glad that she had expected him, and glad that she was pleased to see him ; yet some show of surprise or perturbation on her part might have been a rather more hopeful sign.

'Anyhow, here I am,' was his rejoinder, 'and, as you know that I have only come here to meet you, you won't shut your door in my face again as you did in Paris, will you ?'

'Not for the world ! I apologize for ever having been so rude, but I suppose I must

have had my reasons. What can they have
been, I wonder ? At all events, the door of
Châlet des Rosiers, which is my present abode,
stands open from the time the servants get up
in the morning until after sunset. Bickenbach is with me, and so is Dr. Schott, whom
you may remember. By his advice I am
going through a course of baths ; though he
can't tell me—and I'm sure I can't tell him—
why I should require sulphur baths. What I
do require, and what is doing me an immensity of good, is a course of peace and liberty.'

He expressed a desire to share the fruition
of those blessings with her, and, as she did
not forbid him to do so, they strolled through
the woods together for half an hour ; after
which she dismissed him, saying that it was
time for her to partake of her mid-day meal.
He ascertained the situation of her villa, and
then bent his steps meditatively towards his
hotel, endeavouring, as he went, to sum up
the results of an interview to which he had
looked forward for so many weeks, and which
had not at all resembled his anticipations of it.
In one sense it had been satisfactory enough ;
but upon the whole it had puzzled and disappointed him. The Countess had been per-

fectly friendly, perfectly at her ease, and had
seemed to take it for granted that during the
rest of her sojourn at Luchon they would meet
frequently ; but she had not chosen to allude
in the most distant manner to the declaration
that he had made before parting with her in
Paris, and a lack of courage for which he was
inclined to reproach himself had prevented
him renewing it.   They had simply talked
about trifles like a couple of tolerably intimate friends, which was really ridiculous.
A certain virility and tenacity of purpose with
which this young man was dowered, notwithstanding his genuine modesty, made him
resolve that he would at least not accept the
position of an amiable but impossible *soupi-*
rant.

Thus it came to pass that, on the succeed-
ing day, he betook himself to the Châlet des
Rosiers with a decided step and a mind firmly
set upon the speedy fulfilment of his destiny,
whatever that might be.   The pretty little
wooden house, built in florid imitation of the
Swiss order of domestic architecture, stood in
the midst of a large and shady flower-garden,
through which a brawling torrent, spanned
by several rustic bridges, hurried on its way

down the valley to meet the Garonne. A fat man, who wore a broad-brimmed straw hat, was seated in the garden, smoking a long pipe with a china bowl and perusing a German newspaper. He dropped the newspaper and removed the pipe from his lips, and his hat from his head, as the visitor approached, saying :

'I was about to do myself the honour of calling upon you, sir.'

'How do you do, Dr. Schott ?' returned Douglas affably. 'I am glad to have saved you the trouble of a walk in this hot sun.'

'Oh, the trouble would have been nothing ; I am accustomed to taking trouble. But, to speak honestly, I should not have ventured to remind you of our so slight acquaintance if I had not been commissioned to deliver a message to you from the Countess, who, *par parenthèse,* is not at home. Pray take a chair ; in such weather *on fait bien de se mettre à l'abri.'*

The Doctor was rather proud of his French, which he was seldom permitted to air in the presence of his patroness, whose sensitive ear would not tolerate such methods of pronuncia-tion as *bar barendèse* or *à l'apri.* Douglas

Colborne was less fastidious ; but he did not much like Dr. Schott, who was scrutinizing him with a somewhat sardonic smile, and who, as he was aware, had not failed to notice his vexation on learning that he was not to be admitted into the house.

'Thank you,' he answered rather curtly, 'but I don't think I'll wait, since the Countess Radna is not at home. You had a message for me from her ?'

The truth was that he fully believed the Countess to be at home at that moment ; if so, the chances were that her message would not prove to be a welcome one. However, he was wrong ; for the Countess was really out walking, and the communication which the Doctor presently made to him on her behalf turned out to be of a nature to raise his spirits and his hopes. The Countess, it appeared, had been suddenly seized with a craze for what her physician called *les crandes ascensions.* On the morrow she, attended by her limited suite, proposed to set forth with a view to scaling the Pic de Néthou, which is the highest summit of the Pyrenean range, and it had occurred to her that Mr. Colborne might like to be of the party. Mr. Colborne, it need scarcely be said, asked for nothing better, and was complimented upon his alacrity by his interlocutor, who remarked sadly :

' You have long legs and a light body ; I have a heavy body and short legs. For you it may be a pleasure to scramble over rocks and ice and snow ; for me it is a very great misery. Also a foolish and a most unnecessary misery.'

' Then why you should do it I don't know,' said Douglas pertinently.

' Because I am paid to do it, my dear sir,' responded the corpulent German, with a half-impatient chuckle, ' because I have to be in attendance upon my employer, for whom over-exertion is at least as dangerous as it is for me. What if she were to faint or to sprain her ankle, or even to break a limb, which is a very possible event ? I am compelled to be with her, although you are not, and I shall not be surprised if, at the end of this expedition, she has to remain in her bed for a week. I have told her as much ; but *ce que femme veut !*'

He shrugged his fat shoulders, and, after a pause, mentioned the arrangements which had

been made in preparation for the expedition.
The start was to be effected as early as
possible on the following morning ; they
were to drive as far as the Hospice de Luchon
at the head of the valley ; thence they were to
cross the Port de Vénasque on mules or on
foot, and they were to spend the night 'in
some horrible cavern' on the slopes of the
Maladetta. Beyond that no mule could go ;
so that the ascent of the mountain itself must
be accomplished by the exercise of such
powers of wind and limb as these un-
accustomed pedestrians might possess amongst
them.

'I do not think,' observed Dr. Schott
pensively, 'that the Baroness will climb higher
than the cave ; we shall have to leave her
there. As for me, I can only hope that my
strength may hold out as long as the
Countess's ; for where she goes I must go.'

Such heroic determination deserved a better
reward than the laughter with which Douglas
Colborne greeted it. For his own part he was
secretly in hopes that when the time came the
Doctor might be prevailed upon to share
Bickenbach's lonely tenancy of the cave, and
that it would be his happy lot to escort the

Countess to the summit, accompanied only by guides and porters, who would not understand what they were saying to one another. It was a pleasing vision, and it sent him back to the hotel quite exultant.

CHAPTER VII.

IT will perhaps be permitted to an old climber to doubt whether mountaineering is quite the most suitable or becoming form of exercise for ladies to adopt : he may at least take it upon himself to affirm that they will hardly find its immediate results becoming. However, it is far too late in the day to protest against the participation of women in every pursuit affected by man ; and since it pleases them to hunt, shoot, drive four-in-hand, and actually invade the sanctity of the smoking-room, some of us may take comfort from the thought that we are, happily, not bound to be present when they do these things. For the rest, the Pic de Néthou is not the Matterhorn ; it is not even Mont Blanc or Monte Rosa : it is a mountain of which the ascent

implies little difficulty or danger, though it
does imply fatigue and a certain amount of
hardship. The Countess Radna, to whom
danger and difficulty were words of delight,
was easily fatigued, and hated discomfort ;
hence it may be inferred that her resolution to
set foot on the highest point of the Pyrenees
was due to some other motive than that of
enhancing the high reputation for courage
which she already enjoyed. But what was
her motive ? This was what Douglas Colborne was curious to discover, and this was
what he made so bold as to inquire of her,
while he was plodding by the side of her mule
up the slopes of the Port de Vénasque, a pass
which has to be traversed before the Maladetta
mountains can be reached from Luchon.
The sky was cloudless and the heat over-
powering. Dr. Schott, who preceded his
gracious employer up the narrow path, was
mopping his brow and trying to accommodate
the movements of his unwieldy body to those
of the rough-paced animal which he bestrode ;
a little farther ahead the Baroness von
Bickenbach, under a huge white umbrella,
was sighing and uttering despondent ejacula-
tions in her native tongue ; the army of

porters whom the Countess had engaged were groaning under the preposterous load of baggage which she had laid upon their shoulders. She pointed to the cortège with her small gloved hand, and said :

'Can you ask ? What can be more amusing than to force one's fellow-creatures into making themselves thoroughly unhappy and supremely ridiculous in obedience to one's whims ? The sort of power which belongs to money is an ignoble sort of power, if you like ; but that does not make the exercise of it any the less entertaining.'

'I don't believe you are so ill-natured as that comes to,' Colborne declared.

'Oh, you don't ? Well, it is true that I haven't paid you to walk up this steep hill, and that you are walking up it, when you might have ridden, entirely by your own good will and pleasure.'

'It is evident that if I had mounted a mule I couldn't have walked beside you ; which seems to show that wealth is not your only source of power.'

'You are kind enough to say so, and you mean, I presume, to convey a delicate compliment to my personal appearance. But in

reality I depend almost entirely upon my
wealth : a few years hence I shall depend
entirely upon it. And, when all is said,
it isn't omnipotent. At the present moment
I am in such deep disgrace that, notwithstanding all my wealth, I should scarcely be
received in Vienna if I were to take it into my
head to go there next winter.'

'Yes; I heard something about that,' said
Douglas, with quickened interest; 'Lady Royston told me. I wish you would tell me the
whole story—that is, if you don't mind talking
about it.'

'Not in the least,' answered the Countess,
laughing; 'only there isn't much of a story
to tell, and, such as it is, it was public
property from the first. Count Siedenberg
did me the honour to ask me to marry him,
and as Count Siedenberg is a middle-aged
man of whom I have always stood rather in
awe, besides being quite the most influential
bachelor in Austria, I saw no reason why I
shouldn't accept him. But when I came to
know him more intimately, I found that he
didn't inspire me with awe any longer, which
robbed him of his chief attraction. Consequently I broke off the affair, and the

grandees were furious with me.   That is all.'

'I believe you threw the man over because you didn't love him, and I don't believe you accepted him because he was influential or because you were afraid of him,' said Douglas.

'Is that your view?' asked the Countess, with a yawn.   'Possibly you may be right— in any case, the thing is over and done with; so it doesn't much matter whether you are right or wrong.'

'It matters a great deal to me,' Douglas declared eagerly; and he would have proceeded to explain precisely why it mattered, had he not been interrupted by a request from his companion that he would step forward and reassure Bickenbach, who showed signs of becoming seriously alarmed by the precipitous nature of the incline up which her mule was scrambling.

The shaly acclivity which they had now reached, and which is swept during the spring by constant avalanches, was in truth somewhat precipitous; so that a nervous old lady might be excused for doubting whether she was not in some danger of presently starting an avalanche on her own account by being

hurled, head first, among the boulders that
bordered the track; but, after half an hour
of agony, the Baroness was safely led through
the narrow cleft which is known as the Port
de Vénasque, and forgot her terrors in shrill
admiration of the prospect revealed to her.

There are more beautiful prospects in
Europe than that which is to be obtained
from the Port de Vénasque; but there are
few which burst upon the spectator with such
dramatic suddenness. The step which takes
him out of France into Spain not unfrequently
lands him in a totally different weather-system,
and always presents him with a totally different
aspect of nature, from those which he has just
quitted. The scene which Douglas Colborne
and the Baroness von Bickenbach beheld at
the end of their long ascent was one of wild
and desolate grandeur, partially obscured by
heavy clouds. These hung low over the bare
hills and cornfields of Aragon, breaking up
that portion of the view into broad patches of
light and shade; but the rugged, menacing
mass of the Maladetta, which rose directly
before them, was distinctly visible, with its
glaciers, its rocky slopes and its pine-forests,
devastated by the passage of a thousand tem-

pests and avalanches. Thither the Baroness turned her eyes, after exhausting her vocabulary of adjectives (which, to tell the truth, were somewhat comically inappropriate) upon the colouring of the more distant regions, and when the Pic de Néthou was pointed out to her, she shuddered from head to foot.

'And it is to that frightful peak that you propose to take my poor Countess Hélène !' she exclaimed. 'But, my dear sir, it is impossible ! She will never reach it alive !'

'I think she will,' observed the Countess composedly. 'You, perhaps, would not ; but, then, you haven't my extraordinary ardour for scaling heights. The difference between you and me, Bickenbach, is that, although you can walk from the Avenue Friedland to the Bastille without fatigue, which I can't, I am capable, when under the influence of excitement, of enjoying exertions and privations which you would rather die quietly at once than face. It is your plain destiny to abide in valleys ; and I promise that you shall abide peacefully in the cave of the Rencluse to-morrow until we return to you with feathers in our caps. By the way, where *is* that same Rencluse ? Can we see it ?'

The guides indicated its position to her,
beyond an intervening ravine. It could be
reached in two hours or so, they said ; so that
there was no hurry about resuming the march.
The party, therefore, sat down to rest and to
partake of the refreshment which they had
earned. The afternoon was now far advanced,
for the start from Luchon had not been effected
until a much later hour than that originally
fixed upon ; but although this delay had subjected them to the inconvenience of the mid-
day sun, it did not compel them to hasten
towards the scene of their bivouac, which,
indeed, was not reached until sunshine had
given place to the sharp breath of the coming
night.

In the meantime Douglas Colborne had been
granted no further opportunity for private
discourse with the Countess, who did not
seem inclined to talk, and who, when she
had anything to say, had addressed her observations to Bickenbach. She had brought a
tent with her, besides an abundant supply of
rugs, quilts, pillows and other paraphernalia
which provoked the subdued hilarity of her
porters, and beneath this shelter she retired
with the Baroness, after a fire of pine-logs had

been lighted and the evening repast had been disposed of.

'You and I,' observed Dr. Schott, with concentrated bitterness of intonation, 'may now stretch ourselves out upon the hard rock, beside these very dirty and very badly-smelling peasants, and go to sleep, if we can.'

'We'll get to windward of them,' answered Douglas cheerfully. 'I wish their persons were not quite so saturated with garlic, but that can't be helped, and it's rather jolly sleeping out in the open air ; don't you think so ?'

'I do not,' growled the Doctor ; 'I do not think it jolly to sleep anywhere except in a bed, and, for my part, I do not expect to sleep at all—especially as I have already a most infernal toothache.'

Douglas expressed sincere sympathy, and hastened to add that, under such trying circumstances, his companion ought not to think of attempting the ascent on the morrow ; but Dr. Schott only grunted and flung himself down upon the ground, with his feet towards the fire, after which he set to work to groan dismally at regular intervals.

The groans of the Doctor and the thunderous

snoring of the guides and porters might have
sufficed to keep the young Englishman's
faculties in full working order even if he had
been weary after his long walk, but he was
not in the least so. He lay contentedly
wrapped in the rug which he had brought
with him, gazing up at the twinkling stars
and meditating upon his actual and prospective
position. He was excited and happy, though,
to be sure, he had no real reason for being
either the one or the other. So far, he had,
nevertheless, been tolerably successful. If the
woman he loved, and who was now slumbering
only a few yards away, had not encouraged
him, she certainly had not done the reverse;
he was going to spend the whole of the next
day with her under conditions which must
needs render intimacy unavoidable ; Bickenbach was going to be left behind, and, since
the Doctor's teeth were aching, there was
good hope of his being left behind also. The
most important of the many questions which
suggested themselves to him seemed to be
that of why the magnificent Siedenberg had
been so summarily dismissed, and this was
obviously a question which admitted of many
answers. Answers of a most extravagant

and delightful character invaded Douglas
Colborne's brain while he was hovering upon
the border-land that separates waking from
sleeping consciousness.

He was roused at four o'clock by the head
guide, who was shaking him unceremoniously,
and who, when he had struggled into a
sitting posture, impressed upon him that time
was of value. The ladies, he said, were
already awake and had had a cup of coffee.
Dieu merci! only one of them intended to
undertake the ascent. In explanation of this
ungallant ejaculation, he added that with
women one could never tell what might
happen, and that the weather was not to be
depended upon. ' It may change from one
moment to another ; but, with luck, we shall
reach the summit and return before the rain
begins. Only it would have been better if
we could have set off an hour ago. I did
not wake you: what would have been the
use when Madame la Comtesse insisted upon
making her toilette as if she were going to
listen to the music at Luchon ?'

It was but a hasty and scanty toilet that
Douglas Colborne was permitted to make,
although, so far as he could judge, the

weather was all that could be desired; for
the stars were still shining brightly, and no
clouds were visible. He was joined almost
immediately by the Countess, who was quite
ready for a start, and who, to his great joy,
prevailed upon—or rather ordered—Dr. Schott
to remain where he was and nurse his toothache. Everything had fallen out most for-
tunately: he could not help saying so as he
took his place in the long line which was
presently formed, and the low responsive
laugh of his next neighbour did not fail to
gladden his heart.

The scaling of the Pic de Néthou is like
the scaling of a hundred other peaks—that is
to say, it can be accomplished with perfect
ease by experienced persons, while it is trying,
tiring, and even dangerous, to those who are
in no condition for the achievement of such
feats. The Countess Radna, who was a
delicate woman, and who did not know the
meaning of a snow-slope, proved herself to
be possessed of courage as well as determination—otherwise she would infallibly have
acknowledged herself beaten at the expiration
of the first hour. As it was, she held out to
the end, thereby earning some grudging words

of praise from the chief guide and the un-
bounded admiration of Douglas Colborne, who
perceived quite early during the ascent that
she really had not strength enough for it,
and did not hesitate to implore her to give
the thing up.

It was, however, past nine o'clock when
the final *arête* — known as the Pont de
Mahomet—by which the summit is reached
had been successfully traversed, and the
guides were unanimous in declaring that only
a very brief halt could be safely indulged in.
It would take a good nine hours to get back
to Luchon, they said ; besides which, there
was certainly going to be a thunderstorm
before long, and thunderstorms on the Maladetta were not always amusing.

The Countess, however, vowed that neither
guides nor weather nor any other consideration, person or thing on earth should induce
her to hurry herself. A glass of champagne
which Douglas had poured out for her had
revived her spirits and partially overcome her
exhaustion ; by a chance of rare occurrence
at that altitude, there was no wind ; and she
found it very pleasant to rest upon a sun-
warmed rock, to survey the glaciers, the snow-

slopes, the innumerable peaks and valleys
which stretched away around and beneath
her, and to listen to the congratulations and
compliments of her companion.

'We don't want to be back at Luchon
before bedtime,' said she, 'and if we do get
caught in a thunderstorm, I dare say we shan't
be struck by lightning. Besides, after all the
perils that we have been through, such a
commonplace one as that would be quite unworthy of our notice. Don't you love risking
your life? Little as I value mine, the most
exhilarating sensation that I know of is
placing it in danger; and more than once
to-day I have had the satisfaction of feeling
that a single false step would have made an
end of me—and of you too, since we were
roped together, wouldn't it?'

'Very likely,' answered Douglas. 'I didn't
in the least enjoy the moments that you speak
of, and I was very glad when they were over.
I don't mind risking my life, if I must; but
I can't see the fun of risking it unnecessarily.'

'Oh, what a true Englishman! You are
so phlegmatic, you islanders, that you don't
deserve half the credit you get for your *sang-*

froid. You are born like that; you could not be different if you tried.'

'I suppose all nations are born with national characteristics,' observed Douglas. 'I'm rather glad that swagger isn't one of ours. Nevertheless, to show you that I have some romance in me, in spite of my British blood, I will confess that I would lay down my life for you at any moment, without hesitating, if you asked me for it.'

She stared at him for a moment and then laughed a little. 'Ah,' she exclaimed, 'if that were true ! — but of course it isn't; though, no doubt, you think it is.'

After this there was a longish period of silence, during which the Countess appeared to be absorbed in contemplation of the view. Perhaps she was not looking at it; but, if she had been, it would have deserved the homage of her silent admiration. There was scarcely a summit of the Pyrenean chain which was not visible, from the Pic des Posets, the Vignemale and the distant Mont Perdu, westwards, to the Canigou on the extreme east; the Spanish mountains and plains were veiled by a dark mist which was gradually shaping itself into clouds ; but on the side

of France the sky was serene and the atmo-
sphere as clear as crystal. Everywhere the
colouring had a soft, warm brilliancy unknown
in Alpine regions.

'I wish,' said Douglas suddenly, 'that I
might ask you something.'

She started and turned her face towards
him. 'You are permitted to ask,' she replied, 'and in all probability you will be
answered. I have very little to conceal.'

'Then, will you tell me truly why you
wouldn't marry that Count Siedenberg?'

'I have told you already—what I said
yesterday was perfectly true. My husband,
if ever I take one, will have to be my master,
and it was plain that Count Siedenberg would
not be that.'

'You speak as if love had nothing to
say to the matter. He did love you, I presume?'

'Really, I had not the curiosity to make
many inquiries upon the subject. Oh yes, I
dare say he loved me—as men love.'

'I don't quite know what you mean by
that; but I know how one man loves, and
I can't help fancying that you know too. Is
it of the slightest use? I came out here from

England to ask whether it was of the slightest use, and you will have to give me an answer before I go back. Won't you answer me now and have done with it?'

The Countess raised her eyebrows. 'You seem to have profited by my hint.' she remarked; 'but I didn't say that I should fall in love with a man, or even marry him, simply because he was masterful; I only meant to say that I shouldn't do either the one or the other if he wasn't. I believe I also told you in Paris, with the most brutal candour, that I didn't love you.'

' Immediately after which you mentioned that you would be at Bagnères de Luchon in August.'

' Do you know that that is rather an impertinent insinuation? I am sure you don't, or you wouldn't have made it; and I am sure you must forget that I am an unprotected woman on the top of a lonely mountain. Had we not better adjourn the debate instead of quarrelling here—which would really be a shade too ridiculous, considering that we are bound to descend more or less hand-in-hand.'

Douglas smiled and frowned. ' I suppose I

am very clumsy and matter-of-fact,' said he,
after a pause, 'and I suppose I ought not to
expect everything to be put in black and
white for me. Still, I *should* like to have my
position made clear. What I understand is
that you don't love me, but that you don't
forbid me from trying to make you love me.
Is that so?'

'How can I prevent your trying?' returned
the Countess composedly. 'If you fail, you
will probably be angry and disappointed for a
time; if you succeed, you will, as I pointed
out to you some months ago, get yourself into
quite a maze of troubles. The situation is
not an agreeable one, but you will do me the
justice to acknowledge that I am not responsible for it.'

Whether she was entitled to claim exemp-
tion from responsibility on that score may
appear doubtful to the reader; but it did
not appear so to Douglas Colborne, who joyfully acquitted her and clutched at the straw
of hope held out to him. What she was
certainly responsible for was undue and un-
wise delay at a height of nearly twelve
thousand feet above the sea, while a change
of weather was threatening, and this the head

guide, for one, was resolved to tolerate no
longer.

' *Allons en route !*' said he decisively and
rather roughly. ' If we reach the Rencluse
before the storm bursts, we shall have better
luck than we deserve—*c'est moi qui vous en
réponds !*'

So the Countess raised her aching limbs
with some difficulty, and presently the expedition set forth upon its downward march.

CHAPTER VIII.

THE RESULTS OF A THUNDERSTORM.

To set out upon a forlorn hope and to discover that the hope is not, after all, an
altogether forlorn one is, it must be allowed,
a legitimate subject for rejoicing; and Douglas
Colborne, as he followed his leader across the
knife-edge of the Pont de Mahomet, was an
exultant man. The Countess, who followed
him, and to whom during the progress of the
descent he kept on turning round with words
of encouragement and proffered assistance,
was a good deal less cheerful ; but the
Countess was dead tired, and her thoughts
were, for the time being, of a totally different
nature from his. Most people are under the
impression that it is less fatiguing to go down
hill than up ; but that is because most people
know very little about mountaineering, and

are unacquainted with the agreeable sensation of having a broken back and a pair of broken knees.

'This may be a pleasure,' the poor Countess Radna ejaculated, after she had for the third or fourth time called a halt in the midst of a half-melted snow-slope; 'but it would be difficult to persuade me that anyone can really enjoy it. For my own part, I have had enough of it. I wanted to see what it was like, and now I know. For the future I shall be contented to sit in valleys and pity the deluded maniacs who insist upon scrambling out of them.'

The unfortunate part of it was that she could not be permitted to stand still and bemoan herself. The guides were out of all patience, and Douglas himself, who had not at first been inclined to attach much importance to their prognostications, was compelled ere long to acknowledge that some atmospheric disturbance was at hand. As the day advanced, the clouds gathered and the sky grew dark; suddenly a furious gust of wind swept up the mountain-side, driving the snow before it and almost lifting the pedestrians off their feet; a second and a third gust, each increasing in violence, succeeded it at intervals, and the shelter of the Rencluse was still far away. There was evidently nothing for it but to push on and turn a deaf ear to the entreaties of the exhausted lady.

There was, however, no possibility of escaping the approaching storm. What they did manage to accomplish, before the first flash of lightning half blinded them and the first clap of thunder rattled in their ears, was to reach an overhanging cornice of rock which could not, indeed, be said to afford much shelter, but which might preserve them from being buried alive in the *tourmente* which was certain to ensue. Such, at least, was the opinion expressed by the chief guide, who, remarking that it would be madness to proceed any farther, made the Countess station herself with her back against the rock, but could not induce her to join him in swallowing a glass of raw brandy.

'As you please, madam,' said he. 'You will be glad of it in another quarter of an hour—that is, if we are any of us alive in another quarter of an hour.'

Hardly were the words out of his mouth, when the tempest which he had foreseen broke

forth and rendered any other words that may
have been uttered inaudible. Exactly what
happened neither Douglas Colborne nor the
Countess Radna could ever afterwards describe.
They could remember nothing except the
howling and shrieking of the wind, the
deafening concussions of successive thunder-
claps, the darkness of the air, which seemed
suddenly to have been converted into a dense
cloud of swirling snow, and a sensation of
deadly cold. Probably the worst was over,
when one of the porters was heard to scream
out in an agonized voice, '*Nous sommes
perdus!*' Probably also he had made the
same hasty assertion half a dozen times already
without attracting the attention of his neighbours. But now both Douglas and the
Countess caught his words; and, somehow
or other, it had come to pass that at that
moment Douglas's right arm was tightly
clasping the Countess's waist.

'Is it true?' she gasped. 'Is it true that
we must die?'

He honestly believed that it was. The
storm did not seem to him to show any
sign of abating; he was more than half
buried in the drifting snow; he had, of

course, no thought of abandoning his help-
less companion to her fate, nor could he feel
the slightest hope of extricating her alive
from so desperate a plight. Therefore he
prepared himself, and endeavoured to prepare
her, for what he deemed to be inevitable.

She behaved very well. She was frightened, but she was not cowardly; she retained
full possession of her senses, and, at the pass
to which she and he were reduced, she saw no
reason to refuse him the avowal for which he
pleaded. ' Yes,' she said, ' I love you; and it
was because I loved you that I could not
make myself marry that man. Perhaps, if
we had been going to live, I might have told
you so some day, though I don't think I
should have told you; but it doesn't matter
now. What will happen? Shall we just fall
asleep, or shall we struggle? I don't feel as
if I should struggle.'

Many men and women fancy that death,
under certain given circumstances, would be
blissful. It is impossible to say whether they
are mistaken or not, because the dead are,
most unfortunately, debarred from communi-
cating their experiences to us ; but what is
beyond all dispute is that an anticlimax is a

very humiliating and provoking thing. Possibly the Countess Radna may have been provoked and humiliated when the thunderstorm rolled away eastwards, leaving a clear blue sky in its wake, and when she was assured that nothing more terrible lay before her than a wearisome descent through masses of freshly-fallen snow; but it is more likely that she was too fatigued to concentrate her thoughts upon any subject outside that of her fatigue. At all events, she plodded forward mechanically, in obedience to instructions, and nothing but monosyllables passed her lips until the safe haven of the Renclu·e was once more reached. As for Douglas, he did feel that he owed her an apology; yet, pardonably enough, that did not prevent him from feeling triumphant and jubilant. She loved him, and she had confessed that she loved him : what more could he ask ? He was so modest as to ask her for nothing more just then, and so considerate as to turn his back and move away while she was being enfolded in the tearful embrace of the terrified Bickenbach.

Dr. Schott, whose alarm had been fully equal to that of the Baroness, and who was naturally indignant, now that his anxiety was allayed, joined the young Englishman and proceeded to rate that blameless individual roundly.

'It is fortunate for you, sir,' said he, 'that you have escaped with your life. It would have been very unfortunate for you, let me tell you, if you had escaped with your life and if the Countess Radna had perished. You may congratulate yourself that your folly and imprudence have had no worse consequences, so far.'

Douglas was in too seraphic a mood to quarrel with any blustering German doctor. 'I assure you,' he answered, laughing, 'that I am quite as thankful to Heaven as I ought to be for having preserved all our lives. I didn't order a thunderstorm, you know, and, for the matter of that, it wasn't I who planned this ascent. However, as things have turned out, there's no occasion to scold anybody. All's well that ends well.'

'Who tells you that we have reached the end?' growled the irate Doctor. ' We haven't even reached Luchon yet, and, as far as I can understand, there is great doubt whether we shall be able to cross that vile pass again before night. One thing I will venture to

answer for, and that is that the Countess will
not recover from what she has gone through
without recovering from an illness. You do
not know what it is to be a delicate woman
with a delicate chest and to have your constitution subjected to strains which it will not
bear. Which it will not bear,' repeated Dr.
Schott emphatically and fiercely, while he
thrust his hands into the pockets of his
trousers and nodded at his interlocutor.

Although Douglas Colborne could not
admit that he was in any way answerable
for the infirmities of the Countess Radna's
constitution, he was greatly concerned at
hearing so despondent a forecast from a
competent authority, and it did not occur
to him that the Doctor might have other
reasons for being surly and out of temper than
those which had been mentioned.

' You don't really think that she has caught
a chill, do you?' he asked anxiously. ' She
must be dreadfully tired, of course; but she
will be none the worse for that after a night's
rest, I hope.'

' You talk at your ease about a night's
rest! It is in your power, no doubt, to
obtain a night's rest by merely wrapping

yourself in a blanket and lying down upon
the wet ground; but it is not in her power
to do such things. I cannot tell you whether
she has caught a chill or not; I can only tell
you that it will be very wonderful if she has
not, and that she quite certainly will catch one
unless she can be taken to the Châlet des
Rosiers this evening.'

That being so, it obviously became a matter
of primary importance to a practical man that
the Countess Radna should be transported to
the desired spot by the desired time, and of
this task Douglas Colborne did eventually
acquit himself, though he had some trouble
about it. The Countess, when she was urged
to mount the mule that was waiting for her,
declared at first that she was incapable of
stirring hand or foot, and really did appear
unfit to start upon a long ride; while the
guides, as well as the Baroness Bickenbach,
pronounced themselves in favour of a rest
and a second *al fresco* night. But Mr.
Colborne had a strong will of his own, which
he now thought proper to exercise; so that
he ended by carrying his point. It was, however, a long business, and he had to submit
to many reproaches and remonstrances, both

tacit and outspoken, before nightfall, when he
had the gratification of landing his charges
safely at the Hospice de Luchon. There the
carriage which the Countess had ordered to
be in attendance was awaiting her ; the four
horses were harnessed with as little delay as
possible, and away she drove with her two
companions, after taking a brief and un-
ceremonious leave of the young Englishman,
to whom it apparently did not occur to her
to offer a lift.

She had, indeed, scarcely spoken to him or
looked at him since their departure from the
Rencluse. She had seemed to be half stupefied
by sheer weariness, and he had been unwilling
to disturb or annoy her by anything beyond
an encouraging word or two from time to
time. He was not in the least offended by
the persistent manner in which she had
ignored his proximity; he had understood
that she required a little time to recover herself; he was thankful that she had now the
prospect of a good night's rest in a comfortable bed, and he set forth quite contentedly, with the guides and porters, to
trudge six miles into Luchon in the dark.

' *Ce que c'est que les femmes !*' growled the

head-guide, as they plodded along the road.
'That lady was within a very little of killing
us all this morning ; but she says nothing
about extra pay. As for me, it is not a
hundred, no, nor five hundred francs that
would tempt me to embarrass myself with
her upon the snow a second time !'

But this worthy man and his subordinates
obtained a handsome addition to their daily
pay out of the pocket of Mr. Douglas Colborne,
who was of opinion that the day's experiences
had been worth very much more than that
to him.

It is needless to say that he was at the
Châlet des Rosiers at the earliest permissible
hour on the morrow, and it is almost equally
needless to add that he was not admitted into
the presence of the temporary mistress of that
charming dwelling. He was received by the
Baroness von Bickenbach, who informed him
that the Countess was far too unwell to see
him, but admitted, somewhat reluctantly,
that her illness was not serious. Dr. Schott
thought that she might be able to come
downstairs in the afternoon, and hoped that
the evil consequences which he had at first
apprehended might now be averted, with great

care. 'Only, dear sir, there must be no more
of this climbing up mountains; it is too
dangerous and too exhausting. You yourself must perceive that.'

'I will promise you that there shall be no
more of it,' answered Douglas, not caring to
defend himself against an implied accusation
which everybody seemed determined to fasten
upon him, notwithstanding his innocence.
'I will call again in the course of the afternoon, then.'

Bickenbach, who evidently had not been
taken into the confidence of her employer,
begged him not to give himself that trouble,
and assured him that he would not be admitted
into the house if he did; but he was of a
different opinion, and it turned out that he
was right. Whether the Countess guessed
that he meant to see her, and that he generally
contrived to do the things which he really
meant to do, or whether she herself was
anxious to have done with an inevitable
interview, may be doubtful; but certain it is
that, when he presented himself at her door
later in the day, he was at once ushered into
the drawing-room, where he found her alone,
lying upon a sofa and arrayed in an elaborate

and costly tea-gown. She held out her hand
to him, saying quickly:

' Yesterday is rubbed out of our lives, is it
not ? We start again where we were before
all those horrors happened and scared us out
of our senses.'

He took her hand and knelt down beside
her, laughing. ' What do you call horrors ?'
he asked. ' I was not at all horrified at being
told that you loved me, Hélène, and neither
you nor I, nor anybody else in the world, can
ever rub the memory of that moment out of
my life, you may be sure.'

' That is nonsense,' she returned, swinging
her feet off the sofa with a swift movement
and assuming a sitting posture ; 'it is un-
generous, too. You know very well that,
when I told you that, I thought I was at the
point of death. Now I am alive, which
changes everything.'

' It may change your intentions ; it can't
possibly change the fact that you love me,'
responded Douglas composedly ; 'and now
that I know that, it will be a hard matter to
make me relinquish you.'

She was impressed by his quiet determination, which all her arguments and all the
feminine ingenuity which she employed in

endeavouring to convict him of lack of chivalry did not avail to shake for one moment. She could not deny her love, she could not persuade him that, for his own sake, he would be better advised to bid her farewell and go away, and when he asked her whether she wished to dismiss him because his social position was inferior to hers, she was unable to accuse herself of such ignoble motives.

'Then,' he concluded, calmly but triumphantly, 'there is no more to be said. We shall be man and wife ; we shall be as happy together as two people ever were, and we shall certainly not allow our happiness to be interfered with by mere differences of rank, or wealth, or nationality, or religion.'

' Ah !' she sighed, 'I don't know whether you will be happy, although you are choosing your lot for yourself with your eyes open. I shall be happy, I think ; because, oddly enough, it seems to me that I have found my master at last. I am very tired, do you know, of ordering my fellow-mortals about, right and left, and seeing them run. But I warn you that we shall have some quarrels ; it isn't in a moment that one shakes off the habits of a lifetime.'

CHAPTER IX.

Miss Margaret Rowley, like the majority of
wealthy and unemployed people, had always
an immensity of work on hand, and could
seldom manage to get through half of her
self-imposed jobs in the course of the day.
She was in the habit of asserting that if only
she had time to look after things herself she
would have the very best garden in England;
but this opinion was not shared by her head-
gardener, Mr. Peter Chervil, who naturally
did not like to tell her that her interference
was usually, if not invariably, productive of
disastrous consequences. Peter Chervil, being
an ancient retainer, and having little fear of
dignitaries before his eyes, was not in the
least disposed to submit to instructions respecting his own business from one whom he

still looked upon as a mere child; so that he
and his mistress seldom met without a more
or less amicable interchange of home truths.

One fine afternoon in the month of August
they met, and, in accordance with precedent,
lost no time in flying at one another's throats.
Peggy, who, for a wonder, had nobody staying
with her, and had resolved to devote a good
two hours to gardening, had arrayed herself
in a short skirt, had armed herself with a
spud, and had sallied forth fully determined
upon obtaining replies to several very important questions. First, why were there no
eucharis lilies? Secondly, how was it that,
after all the money which she had expended
upon begonias during the last two years,
everybody in the neighbourhood could beat
her with them? Thirdly, would Peter be
good enough to explain any particular reason
that he might have for allowing two of the
greenhouses to be simply devastated by green
fly? She had other minor matters to inquire
into, but these were the chief, and she felt
that her case as it stood was a tolerably
strong one.

The tall, thin, gray-bearded individual
whom she ran to earth in the potting-shed,

and at whose head she hastened to hurl the
principal counts of her indictment, drew his
hand several times across his unshaven upper
lip before he made any response.

'Euch'ris lilies?' said he at length, with a
smile of pitying wonder. 'Did you think as
you was goin' to have 'em all the year round
then, miss?'

'I don't see why I shouldn't,' answered
Miss Rowley boldly.

'No; that's what you'd expect, I make no
doubt. Same with begonias. I dessay. Same
with pretty well everything. Ah! it ain't
much as *you* knows about gardenin', Miss
Peggy.'

'I know what my garden costs me, at all
events,' the lady declared.

'Do you, now? I shouldn't ha' thought
as you'd have found out as much as that.
Not but what it costs a deal more nor it
ought, and so I've told you many and many's
the time; on'y 'tain't no manner o' good for
me to speak. Well, you'll larn somethin' as
you grow older, maybe. Don't come blowin'
of me up because I ain't the Creator of this
world, and can't play miracles with it, that's
all.'

'Anyhow, I don't expect anything so miraculous as reasonable civility from you, Peter; one doesn't expect a bigoted Radical to be either reasonable or civil.'

The lines of Mr. Chervil's weather-beaten visage relaxed. A change of subject was not unwelcome to him, because the fact was that he had had a little misfortune with those begonias, and he did not wish to talk about it. It is best to pass over little misfortunes of that description in silence, especially when you have to deal with women, who never can be made to understand them. So he said :

'Now, look 'ee here, Miss Peggy: what I always says is, " Business is business, and politics is politics." My business I know, and don't want no man, nor yet no lady, for to p'int it out to me. Politics is, as you may say, a sealed book to me. Consequently, when parties comes askin' me for my vote, I've got to take the word of one or other of 'em as 'twon't be misused. Very well; I takes the word of Mr. Gladstone, him bein', by my way of thinkin', the people's friend.'

' That only shows how utterly unfit you are to exercise the franchise. However, you may perhaps be prevented from ruining your-

self and your country ; and although you are
a very ignorant and obstinate man, you can't
refuse to recognise plain facts when they are
placed before your eyes. Of course you have
never taken the trouble to discover for yourself what Home Rule would mean if such an
iniquitous measure were ever carried.'

'I have not, miss. Have you, if I may
make so bold as to ask ?'

' Yes; and I can make the whole question
clear to you in less than a quarter of an hour.'

This was a tolerably audacious under-
taking ; but it was not through any lack of
audacity, or even of convincing logic, that it
resulted in ignominious failure. Peter Chervil
listened patiently to his mistress's concise
summing up of a difficult problem, and, when
she had made an end of speaking, merely
remarked :

' Well, miss, 'tis not for me to contradict
my betters, and all you say may be quite
correct. Sim'larly, it may not. There's a
many folks, with and without Right Honourable to their names, as don't hold with you,
you see ; and how is a poor uneddicated gardener to judge between you ? Now, if 'twas
a question of euch'ris lilies or begonias, I

should know where I was. But I can't reely
promise for to give my vote to young Mr.
Colborne, miss, though he's a nice young
gentleman and a friend o' yourn.'

'If he were a nasty young gentleman and
an enemy of mine you would vote for him, I
have no doubt. I have a great mind to turn
Radical myself, because then you would certainly support the Tory candidate, and very
likely you would lead the whole flock of other
geese after you.—I am not at home.'

This last assertion was thrown at the butler,
who was now seen approaching along the
gravel path with a fell intent which there was
no mistaking.

'So I told Mrs. Colborne, miss,' answered
that functionary respectfully ; ' but she said
she had seen you in the garden as she drove
up, and she would wait until you came in.'

Miss Rowley sighed impatiently. ' You
ought to have told her that she couldn't have
seen me,' she returned. ' Well, I suppose I
must go. I had several things to say to you
about the garden, Peter, when you interrupted
me by beginning to talk treason and sedition ;
but I shall be out again presently, so don't go
away, please.'

It has already been intimated that Peggy
Rowley was a person for whom Mrs. Colborne
cherished sentiments of the warmest affection,
and these were to a great extent reciprocated.
Still, one does not quite like even one's most
intimate friends to force their way into the
house when one is 'not at home'; so that
Miss Rowley's face, as she entered the
drawing-room and greeted her visitor, wore
a distinctly interrogative expression.

Mrs. Colborne jumped up, seized her by
both hands, and kissed her on both cheeks. If
Mrs. Colborne's manner, which was really a
very perfect manner of its kind, had a fault,
that fault may have been that it was a shade
too effusive.

'My dear,' she began, 'I know I am inexcusable; you didn't want to be bothered with
me, and I have forced you to be bothered with
me. Strike, but hear me. I have had a letter
from Douglas which has startled me out of
my seven senses, and I couldn't for the life of
me have gone home without having told you
about it.'

Miss Rowley took a chair and observed :
'He is going to be married to some fascinating
foreigner, I suppose. I expected as much.'

'How extraordinary of you to have expected it!' exclaimed the elder lady admiringly. 'But, then, you are so wonderfully clever. For my own part, I was no more prepared to hear of such a thing than I was to hear of his having lost his heart to a barmaid. All his life he has been such a good, steady fellow, and has never given me a moment of anxiety.'

A closer observer than Mrs. Colborne might have detected a slight diminution of the healthy colour which graced Miss Rowley's open countenance; but it was in an absolutely steady and unconcerned voice that the latter inquired : 'Are there barmaids in France? and does he propose to espouse one of them? I hope not, because if he does we shall assuredly lose the seat at the next election.'

'Oh dear no!' replied Mrs. Colborne; 'it isn't so bad as that. The lady is the only living representative of a very old family, and is enormously rich, he tells me. She is a certain Countess Radna, a Hungarian heiress, whom he met in Paris last spring. From some points of view it may be considered a great match for him, though it is hardly what I should have chosen.'

'Men have a way of choosing for them-

selves,' remarked Miss Rowley, 'and men who
are worth their salt always do so. I don't
see that you have much to complain of,
especially as the woman is rich. The good
old days of bribery and corruption are over;
still, it does a candidate no sort of harm to be
provided with a rich wife. Free and independent as the electors are, they naturally feel
some prejudice in favour of a man who has
plenty of money and is likely to spend it in
the country. Please give my warmest congratulations to Douglas when you write.'

Mrs. Colborne looked relieved, and indeed
felt so. She had been almost certain that her
son intended to propose to Peggy Rowley,
and almost certain that his offer would be
accepted ; but, since she has been mistaken in
her premises, it seemed possible that she
might also have been mistaken in her conclusions. So much the better : for it would
have been a very sad thing if this unexpected
behaviour on Douglas's part had brought
about a breach of the friendly relations which
had so long subsisted between Stoke Leighton
and Swinford Manor.

'I was afraid you wouldn't like it,' she
confessed half involuntarily.

'I ? Why on earth should I dislike it ?
It is no business of mine, so long as it doesn't
endanger the election; and it evidently won't
have that effect.'

'Oh, but you *are* a friend of mine—and of
his,' pleaded Mrs. Colborne reproachfully;
'his marriage must, I am sure, interest you
a little bit more than the marriage of any
Tom, Dick or Harry whom the Carlton
might have sent down here to stand as Mr.
Majendie's successor.' She added, with a
sigh, 'I don't think *I* quite like it. Money
isn't everything, and this Countess Radna, by
his account of her, is an odd sort of person.
He says she is a freethinker and that she
doesn't care about being married in church,
though she will consent to a religious ceremony if he insists upon it—as of course he
will. That doesn't sound promising, does it?'

'I'm sure I don't know,' answered Miss
Rowley; 'it depends upon what sort of
promises you are anxious to exact. She is a
genuine Countess, and has a genuine fortune,
I presume?'

'Oh yes; she is in the *Almanach de Gotha*;
these Radna people appear to have been semi-
royalists for generations past, like the Princes

de Ligne,' replied Mrs. Colborne with a touch
of maternal pride. ' Still, one doesn't exactly
like her being a sceptic.'

'One doesn't exactly like a great many
things which one is compelled by the force
of circumstances to lump,' observed Miss
Rowley. ' I was explaining to my gardener
when you arrived that I didn't exactly like
having no begonias worth mentioning, and he
was giving me to understand that nothing
prevented me from availing myself of the
customary alternative. If I were you, I
should swallow the Countess Radna's scepticism with a good grace and write a kind
letter of congratulation to Douglas. You
may depend upon it that he will take his own
way, and he will probably be grateful to you
if you abstain from making his way rough for
him.'

Mrs. Colborne could not but feel that this
was good advice. It was satisfactory also
that it should come from a quarter whence
criticism of a less friendly and matter-of-
course description might have been anticipated. She determined to act in accordance
with it, and, after another quarter of an
hour's conversation and a cup of tea, took her

departure, obviously—perhaps even a trifle
too obviously—contented with the outcome of
her visit.

After she had gone, Peggy Rowley sat for
a while beside the tea-table, frowning meditatively at space. At length she rose, stepped
out into the garden through the open window,
and headed once more for the potting-shed.
But apparently she had forgotten the instructions which she had intended giving to her
head-gardener, for when she found him busily
engaged in the operation of shifting a long
row of stove-plants into larger pots, all she
had to say to him was:

' Well, Peter, I have just heard something
which may cause you to reconsider your
resolution as to the next election. Mr.
Colborne is going to be married to a lady who
has plenty of money, and who will probably
spend her money in this neighbourhood if her
husband is elected. That makes a difference,
doesn't it ?'

' Not to me, miss,' answered the old man,
with a swift side-glance at his mistress; ' her
money won't come *my* way, I'm afeard.
Shouldn't wonder if 'twas to make a difference
to others, though. Marriage as you approve

of, miss—if I might make so bold as to
ask ?'

'Between ourselves, I don't altogether
approve of it, Peter ; because the lady is not
an Englishwoman, and I think it would have
been better for Mr. Colborne to marry an
English heiress.   Still, since she is an heiress,
he can't be said to have done badly—and he
has a right to please himself.'

'Right or no right, 'tis what they mostly
in general does, miss,' observed Mr. Chervil
philosophically.   'Men and plants, 'tis all as
one—the young uns can't tell what's good
for 'em, nor yet won't do what they are
wanted to do, for all the care you can give
'em.   Natur', you see, miss—that's where 'tis
—Natur' won't be controlled.   *I* shan't vote
for un—no, nor shouldn't, not if he was goin'
to marry the Queen of Sheba in all her glory :
but, Lord bless your heart ! that don't make
no odds.   The man as you back, he'll get
the seat, miss ; we all knows that well
enough.   And I suppose you'll go on backin'
Mr. Colborne, though you don't hold with
furriners.'

'I shall certainly back him as long as he
continues to represent Conservatism in this

division,' Miss Rowley declared. 'I might
perhaps draw the line at being represented in
Parliament by an alien ; but aliens, I am
happy to say, generally attach themselves
to your party. Mr. Colborne remains an
Englishman, and what does it matter to me
whether he selects his wife from France or
Germany or Hindostan ?'

'Nothing at all, miss,' responded Peter
with alacrity and emphasis ; 'and so I've
always said. "Colbornes," says I ; "well,
come to that, there was Rowleys in these
parts long afore Colbornes was heard of ;
and as for comparin' this here property with
Stoke Leighton, why, 'tis sheer nonsense and
foolishness for to talk so," I says. "Our
Miss Peggy," I says, "she don't need to go
to Stoke Leighton for to find her match,"
I says.'

Miss Rowley's laughter was not free from a
tinge of embarrassment. 'I suppose,' she
remarked, 'that, when you and your friends
fuddle yourselves together at the alehouses,
you are in the habit of discussing me freely.
I don't in the least mind your doing so ; only
you might, in the interests of truth, mention
at the next merry meeting that I have con-

templated marrying Mr. Colborne quite as
little as he has ever contemplated marrying
me.'

She turned away as she spoke, and was
thus spared from seeing the incredulous and
compassionate smile with which her assertion
was received.

CHAPTER X.

AN ACCOMPLISHED FACT.

'I don't see the use of grumbling at him, Loo,' said Phyllis Colborne to her elder sister, in whose company she was drinking tea beneath the shade of a copper-beech one fine afternoon in September. 'We should all have been better pleased if he had been accommodating enough to fall in love with Peg Rowley, and he knows that just as well as you do; but the difference between us and men is that we can't choose and that they can. After all, he might have made a very much worse choice. He is going to marry money—which, I suppose, was pretty much what it was required of him to do, wasn't it?'

'Peggy has money enough for anything and anybody,' sighed Loo. 'I am not grumbling at him — of course there is no excuse for grumbling, since this German woman is so rich—but I *am* disappointed. And the worst of it is, that I am afraid Peggy is disappointed too.'

' I shouldn't advise you to say that in her hearing,' remarked Phyllis. ' Perhaps you might as well refrain from saying or hinting at it in his hearing either, because he wouldn't like it, and it certainly wouldn't do any good. Is that the dog-cart? Yes, there he is, sure enough! Now, Loo, let me implore you to behave like a reasonable being and look pleased, if you can't manage to look over-joyed. We don't want this marriage to bring about any coldness between us and Peg Rowley, remember.'

A few seconds later the head of the family, who had just arrived from the South of France, was embracing his sisters. He wore a slightly sheepish expression of countenance —perhaps an elder brother who has engaged himself to be married must always and inevit-ably appear slightly sheepish on the occasion of his first encounter with his dispossessed relatives—but the letters which had reached him had been reassuring in tone, and he was sustained by a strong inward conviction that his right to please himself in the matter of matrimony was beyond dispute. It was not disputed, even by implication. He understood exactly how the girls must feel about it, and did not expect them to be as enthusiastic as they might have been had his choice fallen upon an English lady of good birth and ample means; possibly he may have had some comprehension, also, of the meaning of Loo's watery smiles, and may not have altogether resented them. Loo was sentimental and imaginative; Loo was pretty certain to end by falling at the feet of the Countess Radna and worshipping her; but there might have been some trouble with Phyllis, who had decided notions of her own; so it was gratifying to find that Phyllis had nothing unpleasant to say.

He had brought a photograph of the Countess with him, which he exhibited, listening complacently to the admiring criticisms which were its due; then he mentioned that the wedding was to take place in Paris some time in November; then he had a cup of tea, and then he went into the house to see his mother, who, as he was told, was in the morning-room writing letters.

Mrs. Colborne was almost always writing letters ; yet, under ordinary circumstances, she would have desisted from her occupation for a short time to welcome her son on his return, and he was so well aware of this that, after he had joined her and had been affectionately kissed by her, he said :

' You don't like it, do you, mother? You wrote as prettily as possible; but I could see that you didn't like it, though I am thankful to say that Hélène was not sharp enough to detect that.'

' I am very glad that she wasn't ; I wouldn't for the world have conveyed to her the impression that I was dissatisfied in any way. Still, I won't tell a fib about it to you, my dear boy, and I must confess that there *do* seem to me to be drawbacks. That civil marriage, for instance. You will acknowledge that it is rather objectionable.'

' Oh, that will be all right; she is quite willing to be married in an English church if we wish it. Only, of course, it would have been absurd to conform to the rites of the Roman Church, to which neither she nor I belong. I suppose what you really dislike is that she is a foreigner, and that we shan't be

able to help spending part of our lives abroad
in future. I don't in the least wonder at your
disliking that; I dare say that, if I had a
grown-up son, I shouldn't exactly covet such
an alliance for him.   Still, it is a magnificent
alliance—if that is any consolation.   Moreover, it is one of those things which have to
be accepted and made the best of, as being to
all intents and purposes accomplished facts.'

Mrs. Colborne glanced at her son's quiet,
good-humoured, resolute face, and laughed.
She resembled the Countess Radna, and, indeed, the majority of her sex, in rather enjoying the sensation of having a master.

'A fact is accomplished when it is accomplished, and not until then,' she returned.
'But the engagement won't be broken off by
you, I see ; and if you are contented, so am
I.   After all, what more can I wish for than
that my children should be contented and—
and prosperous ? It is rather sudden, though.
I should have been glad if you had allowed
yourself a little longer time for consideration,
and possible repentance.'

Young as Douglas Colborne was, he was
old enough to know that nobody ever repents
of an accomplished fact before it has been

accomplished. He did not, however, say this in reply; nor did he see any necessity for telling his mother that the news of the projected match had been received with much less resignation in Austria than it had been in England. There had, in fact, been a good deal of trouble and a vast deal of correspondence; for the Countess had relatives and friends who could not be prevented from saying what they thought, although she could not be prevented from doing what she pleased. But these small and inevitable miseries were no more worth bothering about than the acrimonious remarks and warning prophecies of Dr. Schott. The Countess had certainly bothered herself a little; still, opposition had not served to shake her purpose; she had snubbed all her correspondents, she had quarrelled with a few of them, and she had promised to pension off her unamiable medical attendant. She was now on her way to her native land, where her presence seemed to be absolutely requisite for a time, and in the month of November she and her *fiancé* were to meet again in Paris, there to be joined together for better or for worse until death should part them.

Meanwhile, Douglas also had his arrangements to make, and very grateful he was to his mother and sisters for the readiness with which they acquiesced in the plans which he suggested for their future mode of life. He was, of course, going to be a very rich man— or at least to live like one—but it was just as much a matter of course that his wife's fortune must remain her own and that he would, therefore, be able to do no more for his family than he could have done in the event of his being about to espouse a pauper. He had not been quite sure that Mrs. Colborne and the girls would recognise this, so that he was both thankful and relieved to find them perfectly reasonable. South Kensington was their obvious destiny and destination; they saw that quite as plainly as he did; they betook themselves without complaint and without delay to that task of house-hunting which is one of the most disheartening of all earthly labours, and it was only Loo who presumed to express a hope that they might occasionally be permitted to run down to the old place for a week or two—'when you and your Countess are away, you know, as I suppose you often will be.'

'You pay me and my Countess a poor
compliment,' Douglas answered ; 'we should
like you to come and stay here when we are at
home, if you don't mind.'

He spoke with complete sincerity, although
he knew that there was little probability of
his being taken at his word, and he resented
neither Loo's half-smothered sigh nor her
indiscreet rejoinder. 'Oh, I dare say we shall
pay you short, formal visits every now and
then,' she said ; 'but we couldn't think of
proposing ourselves, or of taking any other
liberty with this grand lady whom we have
never seen. If it had been somebody whom
we already knew ; if it had been Peggy
Rowley, for instance — but it isn't Peggy
Rowley, worse luck !'

To have had Peggy Rowley as her sister-
in-law, instead of the Countess Radna, would,
no doubt, have been better luck for Loo, and
Douglas, being conscious of that, was patient.
For the rest, his patience was not severely
tried. In due course of time a house was
discovered in Elvaston Place which was pronounced suitable by Mrs. Colborne, and after
that she and her daughters were too busy
collecting furniture and preparing for their

move to trouble the head of the family much.

Thus the days and weeks passed swiftly away, and what with making the house ready to receive his bride. ingratiating himself with his future constituents, and snatching an occasional spare day for a game of cricket, Douglas had his hands tolerably full. The letters which reached him from abroad were upon the whole satisfactory; his friends were hearty in their congratulations; the only thing he regretted was that one of his best friends, Miss Rowley, was absent from home all this time. He would have liked to see Peggy and bespeak her goodwill on behalf of the Countess Radna, for he suspected that there was nobody in the neighbourhood of Stoke Leighton, except Peggy, whom the Countess would be at all likely to find a congenial companion. It did not, however, seem over-presumptuous to count in advance upon the goodwill of one to whose kindly interest in himself and his prospects every voter in the vicinity was ready to testify.

During this same period of time the Countess Radna had been engaged in a prolonged battle for independence from which she had not emerged wholly unwounded. She had, of course, been technically victorious, because her legal independence was already established; but the price of her victory had been a downright rupture with several of her highly-placed relatives, besides certain passages of arms in which she had been disagreeably aware of playing a more or less ridiculous part. She hated to be laughed at, and hated herself for caring whether people laughed at her or not; so that when at length she started for Paris, shaking off the dust of her Fatherland from her feet, she was by no means as happy as she pretended to be. She loved Douglas Colborne, and was willing to sacrifice everything for his sake; still, she could not but be conscious that she was sacrificing a great deal. Expatriation, which she had voluntarily incurred ever since she had been her own mistress as a thing desirable in itself, assumed quite another aspect from the moment that she realized how impossible it would be for her to reside even for a short time in Vienna after her marriage : her marriage also must needs deprive her of all the prestige which she had previously enjoyed, save that belonging to wealth. She had been a

prominent and interesting figure in Europe;
she was going to be nothing, except the
very rich wife of an unknown English
country gentleman. Europe would soon
forget her, and the homage of London—if,
indeed, she should obtain that—could hardly
be accepted as a sufficient compensation.
She regretted nothing, only she felt that
sufficient compensation of some kind was
her due ; and she went near to saying as
much when the month of November brought
her and her lover together once more in the
Avenue Friedland.

But Douglas only laughed, as soon as he
understood the drift of her remarks. 'Do
you remember warning me at Luchon that
we should have some quarrels?' he asked.
'Well, we shall have one now if you go on
reminding me in this unhandsome way of all
that I owe you. As if I didn't know that
you deserve to have everything I can give
you! And as if I didn't mean to give you
everything that I have it in my power to
give!'

That was not quite the spirit in which she
had expected to be met; and she was refreshed
as well as amused by his sensible, practical

view of a somewhat complicated situation.
'You are altogether a man, and altogether
an Englishman,' said she. 'You are, perhaps,
right to be both, and to quarrel seriously
when you do quarrel; only you rather tempt
me, who am a woman, and not in the least
English, to show you how easily differences
may be provoked and composed. Suppose,
for example, I were to complain—as surely
I have a right to do—that your family are
hardly treating me with common civility by
declining to be present at our wedding ?'

'Oh, but my mother is coming, after all,'
answered Douglas. 'I told you in my letter,
you know, that they had a lot of work to do
with furnishing ; besides which, there was the
expense of a journey to Paris and back to be
considered, and you said you wished the
ceremony to be as quiet as possible. However, my mother has decided to run over for a
couple of nights. As for the girls, I suppose
you don't particularly care about their putting
in an appearance ?'

'Since you put it in that way,' returned
the Countess, smiling. 'I suppose I don't. I
could even, at a pinch, have brought myself
to dispense with Mrs. Colborne's maternal

benediction. Nevertheless, it is a strange
experience to me to encounter such absence of
ceremony. I have hitherto been accustomed
to a great deal of ceremony, you see.'

' But I thought that was just what you
were so tired of.'

' I am utterly tired of it, and I adore strange
experiences. I am utterly tired of my old
life, and I hope it will be a long time before I
become tired of the new one. It ought to be,
because I feel sure that you are capable of
diversifying it with many little surprises.'

'So long as you don't grow tired of me——'
Douglas began.

' Or you of me—which is, of course, more
likely, seeing that you are a man and that I
am a woman. Either way, we must take our
chance, you and I ; for we don't really know
one another yet. The piquant part of it is
your refusal to let me have the benefit of my
accidental advantages. Ninety-nine men out
of a hundred would have allowed me to settle
a small portion of my superfluous wealth upon
them ; but you are determined that nothing
shall interfere with your privilege of absolute
authority. There, again, you are probably
right, though you are certainly odd. Perhaps

I should not be as fond of you as I am if you were not at the same time so odd and so conventional.'

Douglas could see nothing odd in his conduct with regard to settlements, nor could he perceive the point of those criticisms upon his personal character in which the Countess delighted ; but he liked to hear her say that she was fond of him, and as she repeated this statement many times and in terms warmer than those recorded above before their wedding-day dawned, he looked forward to the future without fear. Every marriage must be more or less of a leap in the dark ; but, in spite of her assertion, he flattered himself that he knew her pretty well, while as for her pretending that she did not know him, that was absurd ; because there really was nothing to know in his case, beyond what all the world might discover in the course of half an hour or so.

Sir Edmund and Lady Royston were good enough to hasten their return from England to Paris by a few days in order to lend their countenance to the nuptials ; Mr. Lindsay consented to act as Douglas's best man ; Mrs. Colborne, who had previously been presented

to her future daughter-in-law, and had declared
her perfectly charming, laid aside her mourning for the occasion, and the civil and religious
ceremonies passed off without a hitch, if without the *éclat* which might have been considered seemly by the relations of one of the
high contracting parties. But as those relations were sulking in the remote distance,
their sense of propriety sustained no additional
shock. The Baroness von Bickenbach was
present, and wept copiously ; Dr. Schott,
secure of his pension, yet not half pleased with
his dismissal, was likewise a grim spectator of
the scene.

A certain great statesman of our own day is
reported to have muttered significantly after
his downfall from power: ' *Le roi me reverra !*'
Somewhat analogous were the farewell words
of Dr. Schott to his departing mistress and
patient.

' The future is not always what we imagine
that it is going to be,' he observed, ' and one
of these days you may again find that you
have occasion for my poor services. I can
only assure you, madame, that while I live
these will be at your disposal, and that, should
the climate of England prove unsuitable to

your health, I shall be ready to accompany you elsewhere.'

The Countess interpreted this saying for her husband's benefit as they drove to the railway-station. 'He means,' she explained, 'that he quite hopes our marriage will turn out a failure, and that before very long I shall be reorganizing my household on the old lines.'

'Then I am very much afraid,' returned Douglas, laughing, 'that a disappointment is in store for your physician. He is a sour-tempered old brute, and I never liked him. Now, the Baroness is really a worthy creature.'

'Yes; but Bickenbach is useless, because she agrees with every word that I say; whereas the doctor, who understands me better, bullies me. If ever I am driven to leave you, Douglas, I shall infallibly send for Dr. Schott, much as he irritates my nerves. I shouldn't think of sending for Bickenbach, who would only cry.'

'Under those circumstances,' rejoined the bridegroom, 'I dare say I may venture to assume that you won't leave me without good cause.'

That she would never have good cause for repenting of her bargain he felt very confi-

dent, and the experiences of his first month
of married life were of a nature to justify that
confidence in every respect. The newly-
married pair wandered through Italy without
ostentation, and with a modest retinue of only
two servants. They penetrated as far south
as Sorrento ; after which they retraced their
steps and loitered along the Riviera, meeting
nobody whom they knew (for none of the
people whom they knew were at all likely
to be in those parts before the month of
January), and enjoying to the full their
freedom from all social trammels. For the
Countess Radna so quiet a mode of life had
the charm of complete novelty ; perhaps also
her husband possessed something of the same
attraction in her eyes. Be that as it may,
she was perfectly happy and contented during
her honeymoon, and did not fail to apprise
him of a state of things which was without
precedent in her recollection.

' What a good thing it is that we can't
spend the whole winter dawdling about sunny
places !' she exclaimed one morning. ' If we
could, we might end by having enough of
laziness—which would be a thousand pities.'

Whether that result would or would not

have followed, it was, at all events, certain that the experiment could not be made. Calls of various kinds rendered Douglas Colborne's return to Stoke Leighton before Christmas imperative, and in the second week of December his tenantry had the privilege of meeting him with a congratulatory address, as well as that of gazing upon the beautiful and richly-attired lady who (having espoused an untitled gentleman) was still known as the Countess Radna. They admired her, it is to be feared, rather more than she admired them. She had been accustomed to a somewhat greater degree of subserviency on the part of her inferiors than is usually manifested in the county of Bucks, and she was a little taken aback when her husband intimated to her that she would be expected to place her delicately-gloved hand within the huge sunburnt palms of various stalwart sons of the soil. She was, however, delighted with the aspect of her future home, which, although by no means a magnificent place, presented that trim and well-kept appearance common to all English country homes.

'This is perfect!' she exclaimed, after a cursory survey of the reception - rooms

'Nothing is wanting, except a certain number of guests, and—an occupation of some sort.'

'We'll ask some people down to stay as soon as you like,' answered Douglas. 'As for occupation—well, there will be shooting for the next two months and hunting until spring.'

'Only, for my misfortune, I don't either shoot or hunt.'

'Very few ladies shoot, even in England,' Douglas observed ; 'but lots of them hunt, and there's no difficulty about it, so long as you are well mounted and have the average amount of pluck. It won't take me many weeks to initiate you into the mysteries of fox-hunting.'

'Oh, you mean me to hunt with you, then? All this is very new and very diverting ; it looks quite like the commencement of a fresh existence. I must warn you, though, that I have already tried many fresh departures, and have always found that *plus ça change plus c'est la même chose.*'

CHAPTER XI.

ANYBODY who has ever tried to teach his
fellow-creatures anything must have discovered that it is not the stupid ones who
give the most trouble. With patience and
perseverance on the part of teacher and
learner, mere stupidity, against which a great
poet has told us that the gods themselves
fight in vain, will seldom be found a barrier
to moderate proficiency ; but of the people
who know a little and think they know a
good deal nothing satisfactory can be made,
and that, in all probability, was why Douglas
Colborne failed to imbue his wife with either
taste or capacity for following the hounds.
She was a very fair horsewoman, but she rode
without judgment and was apt to turn restive
under instruction. Hence she not only gave

herself several falls which were absolutely
uncalled for, and might have had serious
results, but speedily acquired a reputation in
the hunting-field which was not of a nature
to render her popular amongst her neighbours.
Moreover, she did not take to those hunting
neighbours of hers, whose manners appeared
to her to be stiff and chilling at some moments
and far too familiar at others, so that she
ended by announcing abruptly that the pursuit
of the fox did not amuse her, and that she had
had enough of it.

This seemed a pity, and Douglas was very
sorry that she should be so soon discouraged
and disgusted ; still, her renunciation of a
sport which he himself loved was not wholly
devoid of compensating circumstances, and he
had the comfort of knowing that the Countess's
social success, when she was not in the saddle,
was beyond all dispute. The county willingly
did homage to her beauty, to her admirable
taste in the matter of costume, and to her
brilliant conversational powers. As a hostess
she was perfect, insomuch that the friends of
both sexes whom he had invited to stay at
Stoke Leighton (rather with a view to her
amusement than his own) fell down before

her and worshipped her with one consent;
best of all, she quickly won the hearts of his
mother and his sisters, who, as a matter of
course, came down from London to spend
Christmas in their old home.

'Hélène is charming — quite charming !'
Mrs. Colborne declared emphatically to her
son before she had been two days in the
house ; shortly after which Phyllis told him
precisely the same thing, and then Loo
followed suit. The terms in which these
several verdicts were pronounced lacked
variety, no doubt, but that was just what
rendered the tribute conveyed by them such
a striking one ; and Douglas, who reported
the good opinion of his family to his wife with
pride and satisfaction, did not fail to impress
as much upon her.

'My mother and the girls have always got
on pretty well together,' he explained ; 'but
they have never had the same tastes or liked
the same people. That all three of them
should call you charming shows what an
extraordinary charm you must have.'

'Oh no, it doesn't,' returned the Countess,
laughing ; 'it only shows how very easily
anybody can be charming who chooses to take

the trouble. Do you know how to be charming—you, who know so many things? All you have to do is to ask the person whom you want to charm a few questions about himself or herself, and to affect a profound interest in the answers that you receive.'

'But you *are* a little bit interested in my people, aren't you?' pleaded Douglas.

'Certainly I am, because they are your people. Isn't that a good enough reason? If it isn't, I am afraid I can't honestly offer you a better one.'

If this was not too complimentary to the ladies of the Colborne family, it was sufficiently so to their male representative, who naturally did not suspect his wife of exemplifying her theory in his own case, and who was rejoiced to think that all risk of coldness or misunderstanding between those upon whom his affections were centred might now be regarded as outside the bounds of probability.

The Countess, however, could not reasonably be expected to take the trouble of making herself charming to his friends as well as to his relations, and for some reason or other she did not see fit to expend any pains upon

fascinating Miss Rowley, who, like the rest of
the world, was at home for Christmas, and
who called upon the new mistress of Stoke
Leighton one afternoon. It is notorious that
when a man marries he usually finds himself
compelled to drop the feminine intimacies
which have brightened his bachelor years, and
it is likewise proverbial that two of a trade
never agree. Perhaps the good-humoured
Peggy made herself a trifle too much at home;
perhaps long enjoyment of wealth and independence had brought about a certain simi-
larity in the respective mental attitudes of
these two ladies towards their fellow-mortals
which was not conducive to mutual toleration.
In any case, they evidently did not hit it off
together, and Douglas, as an impartial man,
could not but admit that the fault lay rather
with his wife than with her visitor. The
Countess, who could be English, French, or
German at will, chose on this occasion to be
altogether Teutonic. She was painfully polite
and crushingly ceremonious ; she neither
made advances nor responded to them ; and
if Peggy Rowley had been an easily snubbed
person, snubbed she must unquestionably
have felt.

But Peggy, having the great advantage of not caring a straw whether the Countess Radna liked her or not, accepted the rebuff inflicted upon her with undiminished cheerfulness. She acquitted herself conscientiously of her part ; she said and did all that neighbourly civility seemed to demand, and during the latter portion of her visit she addressed her remarks chiefly to the two girls, both of whom had given her a very warm welcome.

'I shall be starting off in a few days to stay with half a dozen different people,' she said, as she rose to take her leave ; ' but, of course, if anything should happen to poor old Majendie, who is very bad, I hear, I shall come home at once and set to work canvassing. You know,' she added explanatorily to the Countess, ' we mean your husband to be our future member. We are going to get him in ; but, in order to do it, we must all be upon the spot at the right time.'

' Indeed ?' answered the Countess, with slightly raised eyebrows. ' I did not know that women were allowed to vote for members of your Parliament.'

' We don't vote ourselves, but we tell the electors how they are to vote, and quite a

large number of them obey us. Your help,
I can assure you, will be most valuable, and
I shall certainly claim it when the moment
for action arrives.'

This open taking of the candidate under
her wing was, perhaps, somewhat injudicious,
but Peggy was too magnanimous to be
actuated by any small sentiment of spite or
any desire to provoke jealousy. She often
blundered in the way that men blunder, but
from the failings characteristic of her sex she
was singularly exempt.

As soon as Miss Rowley had departed the
Countess retired into her boudoir, taking with
her her younger sister-in-law, through whose
arm she affectionately passed her own.

'Tell me about this delightful friend of
yours,' she began, as she sank into one of the
luxurious armchairs with which the room
was a little overcrowded. 'How does she
manage to win elections? and why is she so
kind as to exert herself in this way for
Douglas? She must have great talent or
great influence or great benevolence. All
three, perhaps?'

'Oh, I am so glad you like her!' cried the
unsuspecting Loo. 'Yes; I really think she

has all three, and naturally she is anxious to
do anything that she can for Douglas, because
they have been intimate from their childhood.
She has been kindness itself to us, though——'

'Yes?' said the Countess interrogatively.

'I was only going to say that I don't suppose she can care quite as much for us as she
does for him; but perhaps that would be
rather an ungrateful speech to make. Anyhow, it would be difficult for her to be as
fond of me as I am of her. To tell you the
truth, I always used to hope that Douglas
would marry her,' the girl concluded, with a
laugh.

The lady whom Douglas had preferred to
marry received this confidence without apparent perturbation, but pardonable curiosity
prompted her to put a good many more
questions, to which full replies were forthcoming. Loo Colborne was by far the most
communicative member of the family, and it
was doubtless by reason of that patent fact
that she was then sitting in her sister-in-
law's boudoir. In a very brief space of time
she had related all that the most inquisitive
person could have desired to hear.

'However,' she thought it only fair to end

by acknowledging, 'I dare say things are really better as they are ; for we have gained you, Hélène dear, and we haven't lost Peggy, as I was half afraid we should at first.'

Late that evening the Countess said abruptly to her husband :

' Why didn't you marry the woman who was obviously sent into the world for the express purpose of becoming your wife ? She is not precisely a beauty, I admit ; but she is not so bad looking, and in all other respects she would have suited you admirably.'

' My dear Hélène, you ought to know, if anybody ought, that I have married the only woman whom it could ever have been possible for me to marry. You surely don't mean that you are——'

' Jealous of Miss Rowley ?' interrupted the Countess. ' Oh dear no ! I am aware that you fell in love with me, and I presume that when you did so your heart was your own. What astonishes me, taking all things into consideration, is that you should have escaped losing it to her.'

' Upon my honour, I did escape.'

' Ah ! then you are more fortunate than

she has been. Oh, I hear your modest disclaimers already ; you needn't trouble to shower them upon me. They do you honour; but, unfortunately, they can't prevent Miss Rowley from driving you into Parliament because she is in love with you, or your relations from lamenting that you have been too perverse to reward her according to her deserts.'

' You have taken up an altogether wrong idea,' returned Douglas, looking annoyed, ' and I am very sorry for it, because I hoped that you would make friends with Peg Rowley, who is no more in love with me than I am with her.'

' That is understood, of course, and she shall not be accused of anything so improper again. But I'm afraid I can't exactly make friends with her, even to please you—she is probably too English for me. Political life is very well ; amusement and excitement are to be got out of it occasionally, and I should like, just as much as Miss Rowley would like, to see you in the House of Commons. But all this struggling for votes, this flattering and cajoling of *bourgeois* electors—is it not a little beneath people of our station ?'

Douglas made a deprecatory gesture.

'It may be,' he replied; 'but it is the necessary consequence of a democratic form of government, and I think I have heard you talk as if you didn't much admire or believe in class privileges.'

'I don't believe in any sort of Divine right, and if I were a *bourgeois* or a mechanic I should wish to make short work of the upper classes most likely; only as I happen to belong by birth to the upper class, I would rather be made short work of by these people than stoop down to black their boots. In a word, I am half Hungarian, half French, whereas your Miss Rowley is, as I say, entirely English; that is one reason why I can't oblige you by becoming her bosom friend.'

There was doubtless another reason, and a less far - fetched one; but he was sensible enough to abstain from any further allusion to that, and to resign himself, with a sigh, to an estrangement which he perceived to be inevitable. All the same, he resolved that he would not throw over an old friend because his wife, like many of the best of women, was subject to fits of unreasoning jealousy. Jealousy is a venial offence, but cowardice and infidelity cannot be excused upon any plea whatsoever.

Now, the Countess had averred that she was not jealous of Miss Rowley, and perhaps she was not so in the ordinary acceptation of the term ; she was aware that her husband loved her and that he did not love one who might have been her rival. But what had caused her to declaim against British electioneering tactics was partly her instinctive knowledge that Peggy would beat her easily in that field of activity, and partly her conscious inability to interest herself in the duties and relaxations which were common to Douglas and to the heiress whom Nature seemed to have marked out as his mate. Besides, Miss Rowley was not the sort of woman with whom she would have cared, under any circumstances, to become intimate.

That being so, it was almost a pity that old Mr. Majendie's demise should have taken place with unexpected suddenness that very same night. Upon the receipt of the news, Miss Rowley at once abandoned her projected visits ; a stream of letters and telegrams began to pour in at Stoke Leighton, and although the newspapers announced that no steps would

be taken by either party until after the funeral
of the late member, unofficial preparations
were initiated without delay. The next few
weeks were very busy ones both for Douglas
and his wife: to the former they brought a
good deal of fatigue, not unmixed with
pleasurable excitement, but to the latter they
brought fatigue pure and simple. She did
all that she was asked or expected to do ; she
smiled as prettily as possible upon recalcitrant
voters and their families ; she took her place
day after day and night after night upon
crowded platforms, heroically swallowing her
yawns while she listened to the eloquence of
the Tory candidate and the replies that he
made to searching questions ; but she could
not make out, nor had she any great wish to
make out, what it was all about. Those
queries and answers, which occasioned the
keenest emotion to Peggy Rowley (for
Douglas, as has already been hinted, was not
the soundest of Conservatives), meant nothing
at all to her ; as far as she was able to understand their drift, they did not strike her as
meaning anything of supreme importance to
anybody ; the two things which gradually
became clear to her through all this clamour

of tongues were, first, that her husband was
going to be elected ; and, secondly, that his
election would, in the opinion of all competent judges, be chiefly if not entirely due to
the unwearied exertions of the lady of Swinford Manor.

Yet, as the lady of Swinford Manor could
have informed her, Mr. Colborne's election
was by no means a foregone conclusion ; for
his opponent was a strong man with a strong
following, while he himself was considered a
trifle crotchety by not a few of those who had
supported Mr. Majendie. They did not want
—who does ?—to be represented by that un-
satisfactory being, an independent member ;
and upon more points than one he refused
absolutely to bind himself by any definite
promise. He would in all probability have
been punished for his fads and his scruples by
exclusion from public life but for certain con-
siderations which ought never to weigh with
the constituencies for a moment, and which
always do weigh with them. The Radical
newspapers, when ultimately called upon to
record the defeat of their candidate, pointed
with pride and hope to a diminished majority,
and spoke, justifiably enough, of ' local causes '

as being responsible for their present discom-
fiture; but Peggy Rowley declared jubilantly
that if the electors would return so unmanage-
able a supporter of the Government as
Douglas had shown himself to be, they would
never dream of returning any politician who
belonged to the opposite camp.

'He is quite right to have opinions of his
own, you know,' she told the Countess; 'only
it is a horribly dangerous thing to parade
opinions of one's own before securing one's
seat. However, all's well that ends well, and
since this business has ended well, I'm not
sorry that he has made himself free to play
any game he likes in the House.'

'I, at all events, am not sorry that he has
been elected,' observed the Countess, 'for I
really do not think that I could have endured
many more political meetings. As for the
game which he may have had it in his mind
to play, I suppose you know more about
that than I do: honestly speaking, the game
upon which we have been engaged of late
appears to me to be one of the most tedious
and troublesome that I have ever seen or
heard of.'

It may be that she would have found the

game less tedious if the share assigned to
her in the playing of it had been a less
subordinate one; still, it was quite true that
the methods by which Parliamentary honours
are obtained in England were not such as to
commend themselves to her fastidious taste.

'Since you desired to be made a legislator,
I am glad you have got what you want,' she
said to her husband; 'but I trust that it will
be a very long time before the next election
comes. One needs to recover one's breath
after this, and—and to wash one's hands.'

'I am afraid you have passed through some
most unpleasant experiences,' said Douglas,
with a twinge of compunction; 'but I hope,
as you say, that it will be a long time before
you have to face the ordeal again; and I
think, you know, that my being in Parliament
will be an advantage to you in some ways, as
well as to me. For one thing, we shall have
to take a house in London, which will make
a change for you.'

The Countess brightened a little at this
prospect, for she was in truth heartily sick
already of her husband's country residence.
Stoke Leighton was less magnificent and less
dreary in outward appearance than her own

Hungarian castle, but as a winter dwelling-place she was beginning to find it very nearly as dull. It might be more tolerable during the summer months, she thought. Meanwhile, she insisted that the cost of the London house should be her affair, and he could not very well gainsay her upon that point, although he would have preferred to do so, if he could have seen his way to it. He felt, however, that she had a right to live in a larger house than he could afford to rent or purchase, and to entertain upon a larger scale than his means would admit of; so he yielded to her representations and, as a natural consequence, accompanied her shortly afterwards to a London hotel, in order that she might be able to survey such suitable abodes as were then in the market.

Thus it came to pass that, before long, he found himself master by courtesy of a very fine mansion in Carlton House Terrace, the furnishing and decorating of which detained him in town until Parliament met and put an end to his hunting for that season. The sacrifice of a week or two of hunting was a greater sacrifice to him than his wife could realize, but he submitted to it manfully, and he had his reward in the spectacle of her vastly improved spirits.

'London is not precisely Paris,' she remarked, after their installation was completed and a heavy bombardment of visitors and visiting cards had set in, 'but it is at least not the country, Heaven be praised! Civilized humanity was never meant to live anywhere except in cities or southern watering-places during the cold months.'

'We English don't think so,' observed Douglas, laughing; 'but then, of course, we are barbarians.'

'Well, you are a little barbarous, it must be confessed; still, you are not bad sort of people, some of you; that is to say, that one of you isn't a bad sort of person.'

Such a declaration made ample amends for loss of sport and for the slightly uncomfortable sensation of ruling over a household without paying the cost of its maintenance.

CHAPTER XII.

IT is said by those who are familiar with the
House of Commons and its ways that no
newly-fledged legislator will, if he is well
advised, be in a hurry to address that somewhat peculiar assemblage. His proper course,
it would appear, is to keep his eyes and ears
open and his mouth shut, so that when at
length he does venture to speak he may do so
in such a manner as to secure something rather
more encouraging than the slightly contemptuous leniency which it is customary to extend
to the in experienced. Acting upon these
doubtless sound principles, Douglas Colborne
resolutely kept his peace during the early part
of the ensuing session, despite the reproaches
of his wife, who said she could not understand
the pleasure of belonging to a mere debating

society, which met at very inconvenient hours. To be a Cabinet Minister might be, and probably was, worth while; but to accept the position of a voting machine was to sink below the level even of an English country gentleman.

'*C'est tout dire !*' she added with a shrug of her shoulders.

Douglas observed that Cabinet Ministers, like other experts, had to serve a period of apprenticeship; but she refused to listen to so pusillanimous a doctrine. 'I have known too many Ministers to believe that they learn their duties before they have assumed them,' she declared. 'All they have to do is to make themselves necessary; and no man is really necessary until his friends are afraid of offending him. You will find yourself obliged to start from that point, whether you start now or next year or the year after.'

As Douglas only laughed at this concise definition of the highroad to political renown, she dropped the subject, and ceased to take any interest in public life so far as he was concerned. On the other hand, social life interested her far more in London than it had done in the provinces. Of course her rank,

her riches and her somewhat romantic record
sufficed at once to admit her into circles which
are no longer as exclusive as they were once
upon a time, and which, probably, would not
at any time have excluded the bearer of so
ancient a title as hers: that was no more than
she had anticipated and had been accustomed
to all her life. But she soon discovered that
the British aristocracy, unlike the Continental
aristocracies, which differ from one another
only in minor details, has a certain distinct
cachet of its own ; and this, being more or less
of a novelty to her, appealed to that craving
for novelty which was, in truth, her ruling
passion. She went out a great deal, she entertained a great deal, and she enjoyed herself.
Hence it followed that she was almost always
in good spirits, and that her husband, whose
duties did not allow of his accompanying her
to a quarter of the dinners, balls and recep-
tions which she honoured with her presence,
but who asked for nothing better than that
she should enjoy herself, was generally in
good spirits also; whence again it followed
that he and she drifted by sure, though
scarcely perceptible, stages apart.

It is not very easy to depict the Countess

Radna's condition of mind at this period of her life without doing her an injustice. Tired though she had been of Stoke Leighton, and dissatisfied though she had been with the part of second fiddle which she had been conscious of playing during the election time, she was not tired of Douglas, nor had she ceased to love him. Only she had not learnt to revere him, and she had got rid of the impression that he was one of those strong men whose wives must need obey them, willingly or unwillingly. The course of events had made her once more her own mistress; and in this the course of events was not lucky, for it was really essential both to her husband's happiness and her own that she should be kept in a state of subjection. Of this necessity she herself had, however, but a dim perception, while Douglas, who had the true Briton's abhorrence of psychological subtleties, would have scorned to deal otherwise than straightforwardly with one whom he loved. Moreover, he was rather stronger than he appeared to be, and, entertaining no misgivings as to his ultimate authority, did not care to assert it without cause. He was not less rejoiced at Hélène's unquestionable social success than he was gratified by the amiability which she continued to display towards his sisters and the pains which she took to procure invitations for them which they might have sighed for in vain without her good offices.

' She is a sort of fairy godmother !' Mrs. Colborne exclaimed enthusiastically one day. ' Naturally, she can't do much for poor dear Loo — nobody could; but she is helping Phyllis on immensely, and I feel that I can't thank her enough for all her kindness. It isn't every young married woman who chooses to be bothered with girls, and, situated as I am, it is almost a necessity for me to appeal to somebody else to befriend my daughters.'

' I am sure Hélène is only too glad to relieve you of a little chaperon duty,' answered Douglas ; ' but I don't quite understand what you mean by helping Phyllis on. To what particular good thing is Phyllis being helped ?'

' Oh, my dear boy, you understand as well as I do that there is only one thing to which girls require a helping hand. I won't be such a hypocrite as to pretend that I don't care whether Phyllis marries happily or not, though I suppose you, like all men, are averse to admitting that a perfectly genuine love-match may be brought about by a little judicious management.'

' Oh, that's it, is it ?'

' Good gracious me ! what did you imagine that it was ? Don't let the thought of it disturb you in your study of blue-books, though ; these are women's affairs, not men's. All I meant to say was that Hélène is lending us her aid out of sheer good-nature and kindness of heart. It is very good of her to have taken up Frank Innes, too, as she has done.'

' Yes ; I am glad that she has taken a fancy to Frank Innes,' said Douglas. ' All the same, I trust she won't think it good or kind to stir up a genuine love-match in his case.'

' As if she would be so foolish ! Unless, of course, she could get him to fall in love with an heiress. People do sometimes fall in love with heiresses, as you know, and in a few rare instances the heiress is good enough to befriend her husband's relations simply because they are his relations. I know Hélène wishes to befriend Frank ; and as he isn't a girl, there are more ways than one in which he may easily be befriended.'

This young Innes was the son of Mrs.

Colborne's sister, who had espoused a not very wealthy and by no means open-handed Scotch laird. Frank, the eldest member of a large family, had received a rather more expensive education than might have been vouchsafed to him had it seemed probable, when he was sent to Eton, that he would have such an alarming number of younger brothers and sisters. The cost of his education was a point upon which his father was wont to dwell in explaining the utter impossibility of increasing his modest allowance ; and as the salary attached to a clerkship in a Government office which he held did not much more than suffice to pay for his clothes, he could hardly have managed to exist at all unless the liberality of his father had been supplemented by that of his mother's relations. The late Mr. Colborne, who had been fond of the lad, had been in the habit of helping him out with the annual donation of a couple of hundred pounds, which payment had, as a matter of course, been continued by Mr. Colborne's son and heir. Douglas also was much attached to his cousin ; for Frank Innes was not only a handsome, curly-headed, blue-eyed young fellow of that type which naturally and inevitably secures friends for those who belong to it, but was a fearless rider, a fair shot, and a really excellent cricketer into the bargain. He had other valuable and attractive qualities in addition to these, so that, in spite of his poverty, he was not so very much to be pitied after all.

The Countess had taken him under her especial protection, her favourable notice having, no doubt, been secured in the first instance by his good looks (for it is useless to pretend that beauty is not an advantage to men as well as to women), but also because she had been well pleased and rather amused to discover that he had made her husband the subject of a juvenile and enthusiastic hero-worship. Perhaps she herself was not able to regard Douglas as precisely a hero, and perhaps she was not sorry to find that he could present himself in that light to others. It became a favourite diversion of hers to speak disparagingly of him, for the sake of seeing the young man's colour rise and his blue eyes kindle.

'Oh,' she would say, 'I know quite well what it is that you Englishmen admire: the man who can jump higher or run faster or

kill more birds than you can stands upon a
much more lofty pinnacle in your esteem than
the greatest statesman or philosopher or poet
of the age. I don't think it is true that you
take your pleasures sadly; but you take them
very seriously—far more seriously than your
duties. One of the funniest things in this
funny country is the contrast between the
perfection with which all your amusements
are organized and the slipshod fashion in
which you manage your army, your navy, the
conduct of your public business, and other
matters of secondary importance. What
astonishes me is that my husband should have
deliberately chosen to busy himself with such
trifles. It would have been so much better
to devote his whole attention to hunting and
shooting and cricket, wouldn't it ?'

To remarks of this ironical description
Frank Innes would reply that there were
some fellows who could do anything and
everything that they chose to give their
minds to, and that his cousin was one of
them. He was wont to add, by way of closing
the discussion, that she might say what she
liked, but that when she met with a better
all-round man than Douglas he would take it

as a favour if she would let him know of it,
that was all.

She did not oblige him in that way, but she
liked him well enough to oblige him in other
ways; and it is to be hoped that a really well-
meaning and well-conducted youth will not
be hopelessly damaged in the reader's estima-
tion by the avowal which has to be made, that
she paid a few outstanding bills for him. He
ought not, perhaps, to have taken money from
her; but then, as she pointed out to him, she
had such a lot of money! Besides, although
she was in reality only his cousin by marriage,
her virtual position was much more like that
of an aunt. 'And nobody,' she said, 'has ever
thought of disputing an aunt's privilege to
make occasional little presents to her nephews.'

Whatever this reasoning may have been
worth, it sufficed to overcome the scruples of
Frank Innes, who lived habitually among
rich people, who had much ado to reconcile
economy with that mode of life, and whose
affection for the Countess Radna was not
unnaturally augmented by her generosity.
It was she who, during the Easter recess,
insisted upon his accompanying her and her
husband to Paris, where the house in the

Avenue Friedland stood ready for their reception; and he was not a little impressed by the magnificence of her travelling arrangements, the splendour of an abode which she so seldom occupied, and the high consideration which she evidently enjoyed in the French capital.

'Why, your wife is a sort of princess!' he exclaimed wonderingly to his cousin. 'In fact, I shouldn't think there were many princesses, or queens either, who could do things in her style.'

'Oh, she is very rich,' answered Douglas.

'And she makes a good use of her money, too.'

'Well, yes; I think she does. But, between you and me, Frank, there are moments when I almost wish that she had no more than a trifle of five thousand a year, or thereabouts.'

Douglas did not explain himself further, nor did the younger man inquire what he meant by a wish which sounded a shade ungracious; but the discerning reader will probably have no difficulty in understanding that the position of a prince-consort is not wholly free from drawbacks.

For the rest, the Countess Radna knew that as well as anybody, and was very careful to refrain from hurting her husband's suscepti-bilities more than was inevitable. It was scarcely her fault that she could not help doing so every now and then. After they had returned to London, for instance, and were in the full swing of the season, she annoyed him quite unintentionally, and in a manner which rather surprised her, by ex-pressing her intention of charging herself with the providing of Phyllis's *dot*.

'Why in the world shouldn't I?' she asked, in reply to his somewhat curt intimation that such an arrangement was not to be thought of. 'That kind of thing is done every day in other countries, and I don't think it can be considered so utterly inadmissible here, for your mother gave her consent at once. You pay me a poor compliment by being so proud, and you are not very kind to your sister, either. I presume you have noticed that Colonel Percy is paying her a good deal of attention, and I presume you must be aware that it is just that question of the *dot* which prevents him from speaking out. He isn't a rich man, you see, and probably he thinks

that it would be hardly fair to offer himself to
a girl who might have to submit to privations
as his wife.'

'That is only a pretty way of saying that
Percy doesn't care enough about her to marry
her unless it is made worth his while,'
answered Douglas in a vexed tone. 'I can't
say that I have noticed his attentions ; I
haven't much time for noticing these things ;
but I believe he has at least a thousand a year
of his own, and he will be well enough off
some day. What you say would make me
hesitate to promise a very large provision for
Phyllis, even if I were as well able to do so
as you are. However, I'll speak to my
mother about it.'

He made a point of speaking rather peremptorily to his mother about it ; and the
result of his doing so was not the least what
he had expected it to be.

Colonel Percy, who, before Douglas had
resigned his commission in the Guards, had
been a brother-officer of the latter, was a man
well known in smart circles. There was very
little to be said against him, except that he
was at least fifteen years older than Phyllis,
and that his tastes and experiences had been

such as to render him her senior by any
number of years ; nor could much be urged
in his favour, except that he was heir to a
baronetcy and to a moderate estate.

'It really doesn't seem to me,' said Douglas,
'that Percy is quite so great a catch that we
need feel tempted to bribe him into an alliance
with us—at somebody else's expense.'

Mrs. Colborne was seldom angry, and, as a
rule, either was or pretended to be frightened
when her son spoke angrily to her; but upon
this occasion she deemed it her duty to rebuke
him roundly and soundly. The assumption
that any attempt to 'bribe' Colonel Percy had
been made or contemplated was, she said,
hardly worth refuting, though she was extremely sorry that such a suspicion should
have been entertained. It was true that he
was not what worldly people would call a
great catch ; but surely it was more important that Phyllis should care for him (if,
indeed, she did so, which was by no means
proved as yet) than that he should be a
millionaire. Finally, Douglas might remember that, although he was the head of the
family, he was not entitled to dictate either
to his sister or his wife as though he were

a despot and they his slaves. The one might marry without his consent, and the other, Mrs. Colborne presumed, might spend her own money as seemed best to her without his consent.

'I am not objecting to Phyllis's marrying Percy,' Douglas declared, 'although he isn't exactly the husband whom I should have chosen for her. As for my wife, of course she is free to spend her money in providing the marriage portion — if you don't mind taking such a gift from such a quarter. But I hope at least that you won't let Percy know of your intention and hers.'

Mrs. Colborne repelled this unworthy insinuation with all the scorn that it merited. 'Do you actually believe,' she asked, 'that I am capable of going to Colonel Percy and telling him that, if he will be good enough to marry my daughter, he shall receive a handsome dowry with her from my daughter-in-law?'

Probably she was not capable of behaving with that extreme degree of candour; but she was, Douglas feared, capable of conveying hints which were likely to be transmitted to the desired destination, and she did not

hesitate to avow herself capable of profiting
by 'dear Hélène's kindness and liberality.'
She said that, in the event of her doing this,
she would certainly make no secret of the
matter, nor would any right-minded person
think of censuring her; and she almost made
her son laugh when she wound up by remarking that men of Colonel Percy's expectations
and social importance are not to be met with
every day, even though they may not be
'great catches.'

The upshot of it was that Douglas had to
withdraw his opposition with more or less of
a good grace, and that before the end of the
season Colonel Percy proposed and was accepted. The engagement was cordially ap-
proved of by everybody, except the brother
of the bride-elect, and even he could not
openly disapprove of it, though the manner
in which it had been arranged was not to his
liking.

'Oh, it's all right,' said he to Frank Innes,
who met him with congratulations in the
Palace Yard as he was leaving the House
of Commons one evening. 'Percy isn't a
bad sort of fellow, and if Phyllis is fond of
him, as she says she is, they ought to be happy

together.   All the same, I wish my wife
would be contented to give them a wedding
present of a grand piano, or a brougham, or
something of that sort.   I may be altogether
wrong in my ideas, but it seems to me that
no gentleman or gentlewoman ought to accept
a gift of a large sum of money from one who
isn't even a blood-relation.'

Frank winced and coloured slightly, but
observed, after a pause, that it was rather
difficult for those who were hard up to live
in conformity with so lofty a standard. 'And
I suppose, you know,' he added, 'that the
Countess does consider herself related to your
people now.   In fact, I know she does.   I
dare say you are right to be so punctilious,
and I admire you for it; only, my dear
Douglas, you mustn't expect the general run
of us poor sinners to be like you: we can't
get much further than admiring you, most
of us.'

The Countess could not, in this particular
instance, get so far.   She might have respected
her husband, though she would doubtless have
been very angry with him if he had placed an
absolute veto upon her proposed benevolence;
but she did not think the better of him for

holding opinions which struck her as ridiculous and overstrained in themselves, and of which he did not appear to have the courage.

'For heaven's sake!' she exclaimed rather impatiently, in answer to his final protest, 'let us not talk like a couple of *bourgeois!* You and I surely understand just what money is worth. It is useful, and we are glad to have it and use it when it is wanted; but we are not going to make a god of it, as the middle classes do. If you wish to be very amiable, you won't say another word to me upon this vulgar subject.'

He dropped the subject, perceiving that nothing was to be gained by pursuing it; but he was not convinced that it is vulgar to be scrupulous, nor was he quite pleased with his wife's tone. If he had not had so many other things to think about, he would have gratified her, perhaps, by initiating one of those quarrels which she had once predicted, and of which he had hitherto managed to steer clear.

CHAPTER XIII.

LOVERS' quarrels, as all the world knows, have
from time immemorial discharged the bene-
ficent task of moral thunderstorms, and it was
probably as desirable as it was inevitable that
some few further struggles for mastery should
take place between Douglas Colborne and his
wife—if not upon the question of Phyllis's
dowry, upon some other which would answer
the purpose equally well. But, setting aside
his natural masculine horror of rows and his
political preoccupations, he had a very good
reason for being reluctant to cross her at this
time, if he could possibly help doing so. The
doctor said that, in view of an event which
was not so very far distant, the Countess
ought not to be crossed. He also said that

she ought not to be over-fatigued ; and how
to carry out the latter injunction without
disobeying the former became a problem of
more pressing importance to Douglas than
that of reconciling his sister's acceptance of a
little fortune with his own notions of what
may and what may not be accepted from a
wealthy sister-in-law.

For the Countess, unfortunately, liked
London society, while she hated the idea of
being sent down to Stoke Leighton before the
end of the session. Nor was this prospect
made at all more attractive for her by Mrs.
Colborne's kind offer to accompany her thither
and take care of her until Douglas should
obtain release from his Parliamentary labours.
She ended, however, after a great deal of discussion and persuasion, by assenting to the
proposed arrangement — partly because she
really felt too ill and weary to keep up her
present manner of life, and partly, it is to be
feared, because, like most mortals who are out
of health and out of spirits, she was not unwilling to be furnished with the luxury of a
grievance. To Stoke Leighton, therefore, she
went, attended by Mrs. Colborne and the
girls, while Douglas continued for the time

being to inhabit a corner of the mansion in
Carlton House Terrace.

Now, it may be conceded that if separation
from her husband was a very fair sort of
grievance, as grievances go, the company of
her mother-in-law and her sisters in-law was
an even more substantial one. She did not
dislike any of them personally, but she did
not care about them individually or collec-
tively, and they bored her not a little with
their kindness, their exaggerated precautions
for her comfort, and their unending flow of
conversation upon topics which had not the
faintest interest for her. She wished them
all well, only she wished them out of sight
and hearing; and she looked forward with
some apprehension to the probability of their
spending the entire summer in their former
home.

They certainly talked as though such were
their intention. They had no country house
of their own, and the chances were that
Mrs. Colborne's resources did not admit of
their hiring one; added to which, their
present quarters suited them admirably, being
within easy reach of Windsor, where Colonel
Percy was quartered. Although nothing had

been said about it, there seemed to be a tacit
understanding that the wedding, which was
to take place in the autumn, would be solem-
nized at the parish church, and that the bride
would be married from her brother's house.
That sort of thing, the Countess sometimes
reflected in moments of ill-temper, is scarcely
the reward that one is entitled to expect for
having shown one's self amiable as well as
generous.

Colonel Percy, who was always coming
over to luncheon, was a rather dull man ;
Phyllis, though grateful and affectionate, was
reserved. The pair did not, after all, seem to
be passionately in love with one another. It
was impossible to feel any great interest in
them, and not easy even to participate in the
excitement which attended the purchase of
the trousseau. The Countess was, perhaps,
too rich to care as much as women generally
do about *chiffons;* at any rate, she did not
care about them, preferring to leave such
matters to her dressmakers, her tailors and
her maids. More than once she had vague
thoughts of decamping at a moment's notice—
so as to avoid argument—and telegraphing to
her husband to join her somewhere on the

Continent. More than once, too, she caught herself sighing for Bickenbach, who at least understood her and her moods, though she *was* such an old goose.

Matters mended a little, but only a little, when worn-out legislators were dismissed for their holidays and when Douglas arrived, rejoicing at the prospect of once more donning his cricketing flannels. It is true that the Countess altogether failed to understand the fun of cricket, even after she had witnessed a match and after all its details had been fully and laboriously explained to her ; it is true that to hear cricket, and scarcely anything else, talked about from morning to night is a little trying to anybody who does not play the game ; still, she was glad to have her husband back, and glad also that he had brought Frank Innes with him. Frank Innes was the one of Douglas's relations whom she liked by far the best. Frank was not wholly given up to sports and pastimes ; he could talk, for instance, about music, and was just now very willing to do so, having recently discovered, to his great delight, that he possessed a pure tenor voice, which he was cultivating with great assiduity. Frank was one of those young men who are always ready to bestow immense pains upon any kind of work which is not compulsory.

'I'll tell you what it is,' he said one day to the Countess, with whom he was now upon terms of the most confidential intimacy ; 'I shouldn't wonder a bit if I were to turn out a second Sims Reeves some fine morning. I was talking last week to a professional chap, and he told me that the quality of my voice was pretty nearly perfect. To sing a couple of songs at a hundred pounds apiece on Tuesdays and Thursdays during the season, and to have the rest of one's time free for innocent diversions, would be about good enough, wouldn't it ?'

'I am not sure that it would be good for you to have too much free time, or that all your diversions would be innocent,' she answered, laughing ; 'but if Heaven has blessed you with a talent or a faculty of any kind, you certainly ought to utilize it. Unhappily for me, Heaven has seen fit to deny me exceptional talents and faculties.'

'That's quite as it should be. Having granted you exceptional beauty and an exceptionally big fortune and the very best husband

in the world, Heaven has done more than
enough for you, in my humble opinion. I
used to think Miss Rowley the luckiest
woman of my acquaintance; but you can
walk right away from her. Of course she
isn't in the same class with you as far as
beauty goes, and I don't suppose she is a
quarter as rich; moreover, she hasn't had the
good-fortune to marry Douglas.'

'Well, no, she hasn't married him, but she
doesn't allow that trifling omission to deter
her from treating him as if he belonged to her.
She was here the other day, and she couldn't
have given him more orders or instructions if
she had been his sole constituent. I suppose,
living where I do, it would be an abominable
heresy to say openly that I don't like Miss
Rowley; but, as I am sure you won't betray
me, I may confess in strict confidence to you
that she is rather too well pleased with herself
to please me.'

'Oh, you would like her if you knew her
better,' answered Frank. 'I dare say she may
seem to you to be a bit dictatorial, but she
doesn't mean to be, and she can't very well
help seeming so; because, after all, she does
rule the roast hereabouts, you know. Besides,

all things considered, I should think you
could afford to be generous to her.'

That was just what the Countess was not
so certain about. No doubt, other things
being equal, she could (as Frank Innes might
have expressed it) have given Peggy Rowley
points and a beating in respect to beauty and
fortune; but the inequality of other things
was more manifest to her than it was to her
juvenile confidant. She was convinced, and
perhaps rightly convinced, that nothing but
the accident of having spent an Easter holiday
in Paris had prevented Douglas from espous-
ing his well-to-do neighbour. She could not
but be aware that Peggy would have proved
a more suitable helpmate for him than she
herself could ever be ; and, although her trust
in him was not shaken, she did not absolutely
trust Miss Rowley. It stood to reason that
Miss Rowley must be a disappointed woman,
and one does not need to be a sorceress in
order to divine what course a disappointed
woman is likely to pursue under certain circumstances.

Now, it came to pass that, in accordance
with custom and precedent, Miss Rowley gave
a garden-party at this time, and that the

Countess Radna, amongst others, honoured the Swinford Manor festivities with her presence. The honour was duly appreciated, and the Countess was duly admired ; but English people when in the country are apt to be too shy or too lazy to conduct themselves exactly as they would do in London drawing-rooms, and thus it often happens that strangers find their welcome a somewhat chilling one. The Countess, after the first few minutes, was disagreeably conscious of being left out in the cold. Two or three dowagers sat down beside her, and, with an obvious effort, pumped up commonplaces from the recesses of their minds for her benefit ; but these ladies were so silly and so tedious that she ruthlessly scared them away, and her hostess's middle-aged duenna, who hovered near her, looking anxious and apprehensive, was a poor substitute for the knot of young people who had congregated round Douglas and were chattering and laughing together like so many happy children. The Countess would have liked to join the group, but did not choose to do so uninvited, and she appeared to have been forgotten both by her husband and by Peggy Rowley, who at

that moment was impressing emphatically
upon him the paramount importance of his
making a big score at the approaching county
cricket-match.

'I don't grumble at you for not having
electrified the House by your eloquence yet,'
the Countess heard her say ; 'you are right to
bide your time.   But it is as clear as daylight
that you must do *something* to win popular
esteem ; and if you were to get bowled first
ball, I should tremble for your chances at the
General Election—which may come any day,
mind you.'

The listener overheard several more speeches
of this half-serious, half-jocular description,
and was not best pleased with any of them.
It must be acknowledged that if she had been
pleased, or even if she had not been slightly
provoked, she would have been a rather
abnormal sort of wife.   The absurd part of it
(that, at least, was what she felt) was that all
these good people who were turning their
backs upon her were so essentially her
inferiors.   Anywhere on earth, except in England, they would have been bowing down
before her, while she would have been exerting
herself with her accustomed graciousness and

affability to set them at their ease. The experience through which she was passing had the advantage of novelty; but it had the disadvantage of being novel in quite the wrong direction. To be tired of being a spoilt child is probably the destiny of all Fortune's spoilt children; but it does not follow that their longing for a little change is at all likely to be gratified by neglect, and the half-hour of undisturbed meditation which was accorded to the Countess Radna convinced her that change of another kind was what she required.

' Do you know what I am going to do ?' she said abruptly to her husband, as he was driving her along the road towards Stoke Leighton in a mail-phaeton, his mother and sisters following in the family barouche. ' I am going home to Hungary. Hungary isn't so very much home, you may say. Well, I grant you that; still, when one is reduced to a choice of evils, one naturally selects the less. I wouldn't for the world say that there is anything intrinsically evil about this rural abode of yours, or about Mrs. Colborne, or Phyllis, or Loo, or Miss Rowley, or cricket matches or garden-parties ; only it so happens that all these people and things present themselves to

me in an unmistakably evil light for the
moment. Set it down to my state of health,
if you like—I shall not contradict you.'

'But, my dear Hélène,' objected Douglas,
whose countenance had fallen considerably
during the above outburst, 'it is precisely
your state of health which puts such a journey
out of the question for the present. I am
sorry, though I am not surprised, at your
disliking English country life, and later in the
year I will take you to Hungary with pleasure
if you still wish it, but I don't see how the
thing could possibly be done now—I don't,
really.'

'I do. It can be done by the simple expe-
dient of sending off a few telegrams and taking
a few railway tickets. There are doctors in
Vienna as well as in London ; there is one
of the name of Schott, who is thoroughly
acquainted with my constitution, and will be
only too pleased to obey any summons from
me. Nothing that I know of prevents our
leaving England the day after to-morrow—
unless, indeed, it be the necessity of your
acquiring political distinction by running to
and fro seventy or eighty times between one
bunch of little sticks and another.'

Douglas laughed a little uneasily. 'Oh, of course the cricket doesn't matter,' said he; 'but there's Phyllis's wedding, you know. If you mean, as I suppose you do, that we are to domicile ourselves in Hungary for the next three months or so, we shouldn't be back in time for that.'

'I should sincerely regret our enforced absence, but I imagine that the bride and bridegroom would contrive to get married quite comfortably without us. In a word, we are not wanted here, and one of us doesn't want to be here; the only question is whether the other is unselfish enough to tear himself away. Don't trouble to tell me that I am unreasonable and capricious; all that is understood and admitted. But when every admission has been made, the fact still remains that I am at the end of my patience. If you won't take flight with me, I shall have to take flight alone.'

Douglas Colborne was blessed with a very fairly even temper, and could control himself as well as most men ; but, of course, he did think his wife capricious and unreasonable, though he refrained from saying so. He conjectured that she must have been put out by

something which had occurred at the garden-
party, and he judged it best not to question
her, but merely to beg that she would take
another twenty-four hours for consideration.

'If you are still in the same mind this time
to-morrow, and if the doctor doesn't absolutely
forbid it, we will do as you wish,' he said.
'Only I must confess that I shall be very
much astonished if the doctor doesn't forbid
it.'

The Countess rejoined that she was not
inclined to acknowledge herself the slave of
any doctor ; whereupon her husband made a
slight grimace, touched up the horses with
his whip and held his tongue.

In the course of the evening he consulted
his mother, who lifted up her hands and her
voice in dismay, and was for betaking herself
to dear Hélène's bedroom immediately and
reasoning with her ; but this Douglas somewhat peremptorily forbade, remarking that
the case was not one in which counsels of
reason were likely to be of much avail.

'What I can't quite make up my mind
about,' he added, 'is whether I ought to say
Yes or No ; and it looks to me rather as if I
should have to say Yes.'

'Oh, but you *can't!*' remonstrated Mrs. Colborne. 'After having made all your arrangements for the summer and autumn, it would be too ridiculous, besides being most imprudent and foolish, to upset them in obedience to a mere whim, which will pro- bably pass in a day or two. Pray don't bother yourself any more, but leave Hélène to me. You might allow me credit for having had some experience of these things and for knowing a little more about them than you can.'

That sounded plausible, and Douglas with- drew a veto which, as he could not but be aware, had small chance of being respected, whether he withdrew or maintained it; but on the ensuing morning the Countess's maids received instructions to pack up, and soon after breakfast his mother sought him out with a crestfallen mien and a confession of defeat.

'Dear Hélène is most kind and thoughtful,' the good lady said ; 'she begs us not to dis- turb ourselves in any way on her account, and hopes, as I am sure you do too, that we shall remain here until after the wedding, just as if we had you with us. But she won't

hear of abandoning this journey; she won't
even listen to any discussion of the subject.
I don't quite know how Hélène manages it,'
added Mrs. Colborne candidly; ' but she has
a way of making one understand that, when
her mind is made up, it would be almost
impertinent to argue with her. Perhaps,
after all, the risk won't be so very great.
However, we shall see what the doctor says.'

It was at all events evident that Mrs.
Colborne's matronly alarm and maternal
solicitude had been lulled to rest by that unscrupulous bribe of free board and lodging for
the remainder of the summer months; and
Douglas, perceiving this, was amused in spite
of his annoyance. He was naturally rather
annoyed at being dragged off to Hungary
without rhyme or reason just as the prospect
of a period of holiday-making had seemed to
lie open to him; but he was not altogether
blind to the petty vexations from which his
wife was determined to escape, nor did he
think that he would be justified in opposing
her fancies, so long as the doctor's consent
could be obtained to the fulfilment of them.

The local practitioner, it need scarcely be
said, sanctioned everything that he was told

to sanction, merely recommending certain precautions which would have been taken without his orders, and the Countess scored a
victory which was not much the less a victory
because it was only won upon sufferance. A
strong man can afford, and is sometimes right,
to yield a point against his better judgment;
but he may be perfectly certain that, when-
ever he does this, his strength will be
accounted as weakness by the other sex.

The first stage of the journey undertaken
by Douglas Colborne and his wife landed
them no farther on their way than their own
house in London. The Countess, who was in
high good-humour, was willing to submit
to all trifling restrictions, and did not
in the least mind spending a week over a
transit which might have been accomplished
in a third of that time : provided that she
was delivered from Mrs. Colborne and the
girls and Peggy Rowley, the rest was a
matter of indifference to her—or, at least, that
was what she imagined.

'I am truly sorry for you,' she said in a
half-mocking tone to her husband, as they sat
down to dinner together on the first evening,
'but what would you have? *Ce que femme*

veut, Dieu veut; and, to tell you the truth, those excellent relations and friends of yours were beginning to get upon my nerves in an insupportable manner. I really couldn't have endured them another day.'

She might have crowed over him a little less defiantly, he thought ; but he kept his temper and held his tongue. Unluckily, that did not satisfy her. She wanted whatever it is (the present narrator does not know what it is, and therefore will not attempt to say) that women want when they insist upon provoking unnecessary squabbles ; she was resolved to make him angry ; she laughed at the docility with which he had allowed himself to be placed in political leading-strings by a lady whose manners and appearance she satirized freely ; she inquired whether he had obtained that lady's permission to absent himself from home, and at length she irritated him into retorting :

'Upon my word, Hélène, you would do better to imitate Peggy Rowley in some respects than to sneer at her. She may not be your style, but that doesn't prevent her from being, and well deserving to be, one of the most popular women in England. At

any rate, there is nothing small or shabby
about her ; and I'm quite sure that if she
hated you as much as you seem to hate
her, she wouldn't say nasty things about you
behind your back.'

Well, the Countess had gained her point,
and, as so frequently happens in such cases,
had got rather more than she had bargained
for or desired. Douglas was not a satisfactory
man to quarrel with ; anger, which was not a
transient emotion with him, made him cool
instead of hot, and so it came to pass that the
ensuing encounter proved a more serious one
than the aggressor had intended it to be.
Upon the details of it there is no need to
dwell. Most of us, unhappily, know only too
well that, whether we remain cool or boil over
under provocation, we usually, in the thick of
the strife, say things which we afterwards
regret ; and if Douglas sinned less than his
wife in this respect, the chances are that he
was not a great deal less aggravating. But
be that as it may, she retired to her bedroom
at length in tears, and without having
achieved the hoped-for reconciliation, while
he betook himself to his study, to wonder
moodily, over a cigar, whether, in marrying

as he had done, he had not, perhaps, undertaken a task somewhat too complicated for
the average straightforward Briton to cope
with.

He had smoked a second and a third cigar
before an agitated tap at his door was followed
by the entrance of the Countess's maid, who
came to announce that her mistress had been
taken very ill indeed, and that she thought a
doctor ought to be summoned. That this
was a step which must be taken without
delay Douglas perceived as soon as he had
run upstairs, two steps at a time; but that
medical skill is of little avail after Nature has
caught the bit between her teeth he was
destined to be made aware in the small hours
of the morning, when a son was born to
him, who only survived his birth by a few
minutes.

'It is very unfortunate, Mr. Colborne,' said
the experienced personage who imparted these
sad tidings to him; 'but we may well be
thankful that things are no worse. I am glad
to be able to tell you that, so far as can be
seen at present, the Countess Radna's life is
not in danger. Some danger, of course, there
is, and must be; only there might have been

a great deal more. You cannot have forgotten my warning you that absolute rest and immunity from worry of any kind would be found essential in her case.'

It was thus that Douglas, like many a comparatively innocent man before him, was humbled to the dust by a sense of inexcusable guilt.

CHAPTER XIV.

CUTTING THE KNOT.

SMALL things, whether they be joys or sorrows, pass out of sight and are forgotten as soon as they come into rivalry with great ones, and Douglas Colborne had no need to reproach himself for a catastrophe which his wife never dreamt of attributing even remotely to his sternness. Nevertheless, he did reproach himself, his penitence being in no wise diminished by the evident sincerity with which, when she was able to talk again, she assured him that she was unconscious of having anything to forgive. It is true that he had some reason for doubting whether he had been really and truly forgiven ; because it is difficult for a man to understand why the death of an infant who can scarcely be said to have ever lived should be the cause for more than a transient emotion of grief, and because the Countess, although she recovered her health as rapidly as could have been expected, did not recover her spirits. In certain respects one of the sexes must always remain a mystery to the other; perhaps also the honest inability of men to enter into the feelings of women is answerable for a large proportion of those estrangements regarding which it is customary for bystanders to affirm that there is no fault on either side.

Such an estrangement now sprang up gradually between Douglas and his wife, and was more or less recognised and deplored by both of them—by him, it may be, rather more than by her. They did not fall out again—it would probably have been much better for them if they had—they were perfectly good friends and did their best to consult one another's comfort and convenience, but each became conscious of a loss of sympathy which was not very likely to be regained. In a word, they had witnessed the inevitable extinction of romantic love, while that kind of love which ought always to be ready to take its place at the right moment had somehow failed to put in an appearance. Douglas, as

men, when confronted with this universal experience, invariably do, shut his eyes to the
truth ; the Countess, as women (perhaps in
this instance alone) generally do, looked it in
the face and, as they very seldom do, shrugged
her shoulders and smiled at it.

When she was well enough to travel, he
took her to her ancestral domain in Hungary.
She expressed a desire to carry out the interrupted programme, and of course he asked
nothing better than to comply with any wish
of hers which seemed to hold out a prospect
of restoring her vanished cheerfulness. But
Hungary did not produce that effect upon her;
nor did the shooting - parties and festivities
which were organized for his benefit exhilarate
him. Something was wrong which certainly
could not be set right by means of novel experiences, or sport, or by the splendid hospitality
of neighbouring magnates, who, notwithstanding their hospitality, made it manifest, either
designedly or because they could not help
themselves, that the Countess Radna's husband was not in their eyes the Countess Radna's
equal. The Right Honourable Douglas Colborne—to give him the full style and title to
which he may lay claim to-day—will always

retain a genuine liking and admiration for the
Hungarian nobility, who, he says, are as good
sportsmen and as good fellows as if they had
been born Englishmen; but it is most improbable that he will ever care to renew his
acquaintanceship with them in their native
land.

He bade them farewell, with no very profound sentiments of regret, in the month of
November, by which time his wife had signified to him that she also had had enough of
her compatriots. She might have added, but
did not add, that she had had enough of his,
into the bargain; she might have told him,
but did not tell him, that she was longing to
pass the winter in some sunny Southern resort
and dreaded the idea of a return to Stoke
Leighton. It was no fault of his that he was
unable to divine sentiments so completely at
variance with his own; nor, on the other
hand, was it any fault of hers that her husband's country residence, when its doors were
once more thrown open to admit her, struck
her as almost unendurably dull, dreary and
forlorn. Some consolation, to be sure, might
be derived from the thought that its dulness
and dreariness were no longer enlivened by the

presence of Mrs. Colborne and her daughters;
for one of these ladies was now safely married,
while the other two were as safely domiciled
in their London home. Still, the outlook in
that cold, gray, cheerless weather was far
from being a joyous one, and the Countess's
heart sank as she endeavoured to steel herself
to the duty of facing it.

'Oh no, I am not going to hunt again,' she
said, in reply to an early suggestion on
Douglas's part ; 'but don't let that prevent
you from following the hounds. In fact, I
can't see what alternative is open to you,
except suicide.'

It was to speeches of that description that
Douglas could find no adequate rejoinder.
Did she mean that she wanted him to ex-
patriate himself, or was it that she cherished
a smouldering but unquenchable feeling of
resentment against him for having once addressed her roughly at a critical moment, and
that, do what he would, she would never
be able to live happily with him again?
Either way, silence and patience seemed the
safest remedies to trust to, since he had
already expressed and given evidence of his
repentance, and since he could not turn his

back upon England, even to please her. So he took to hunting three days a week, and often forgot his troubles in the joy of riding straight, as well as risking his neck every now and again.

He was thus employed one afternoon, and the Countess was, as usual, absolutely unemployed, when who should drive up to the door to pay a neighbourly call but Miss Margaret Rowley! She was admitted, no instructions to turn away visitors having been given to the butler, and she was received with somewhat less of formality than she had anticipated on hearing that the Countess Radna was at home. The Countess was, in truth, so unspeakably bored that she could not for the life of her help welcoming a lady who, in her opinion, was rather too ready to count as a right upon being welcomed. Besides, there were points as to which she felt a certain degree of curiosity which Miss Rowley was presumably in a position to allay; consequently, she did not trouble herself to beat about the bush, but, after she had rung the bell and ordered tea, began:

'You have known my husband from his infancy, I believe. I wish you would be kind enough to tell me candidly what you think of him.'

Miss Rowley stared for a moment and then laughed. 'It is lucky,' she remarked, ' that I think nothing but good of him; for if I happened to think him a scoundrel or a fool, I could hardly say so, could I?'

' But, as it would be impossible for you to think him either the one or the other, my question isn't an unanswerable one. Of course, I shouldn't have put it if it had been.'

' All the same I don't know that I can answer it,' said Peggy, after a short pause ; ' one doesn't care to tell all the thoughts that one has about one's friends. Speaking broadly, I should say that I think Douglas Colborne an excellent specimen of the average English gentleman. He is excellent, I mean, because he has all the average English gentleman's good qualities and a considerably larger share of brains. Will that do?'

' Yes, if you will not be induced to say more. But it would be more interesting if you were to take into account, as you naturally must when you think about him at all, that he is an English gentleman who has placed himself by his marriage in a very unusual situation. What do you suppose he is going to make out of that situation ?'

'Doesn't that depend at least as much upon you as upon him ?' asked Peggy in return. 'I am sure that he will always behave as a gentleman should; but that is really the limit of my knowledge upon the subject. I know no more than that he has married a foreigner, who is also a great lady in her own country, and that in such cases there is probably need for a good deal of giving and taking on both sides. But it is Douglas's nature to give rather than to take ; so it should be easy to live with him.'

'Ah, that is really interesting ! So a person who is more willing to give than to take is your idea of an easy person to live with ? I should have said just the contrary ; but that only shows how useful it is to compare notes with other people. Douglas, as you are evidently aware, will take nothing ; I wonder how much he would give, supposing that he were driven into a corner.'

The entrance of the butler, attended by a couple of satellites, bearing a tea-table, a kettle and other paraphernalia, gave Miss Rowley time to consider what response it

behoved her to make to the above challenge.
When she and her entertainer were once more
left to themselves, she said:

'I should be sorry to drive him into a
corner; the most pacific of Englishmen will
show fight if he is treated in that way. I
haven't the slightest idea of what it is that
you are alluding to; only, as you ask me
what I think of a man whom I have known
intimately all my life, I needn't hesitate to
say that I think he should be taken seriously.
It would be a hazardous sort of experiment,
which he wouldn't understand, to make
extravagant demands upon him merely for
the sake of discovering whether he would
yield to them or not.'

'If, for example, I were to beg him to take
me out of this dismal climate to the Riviera
for the rest of the winter?'

'Oh, I have no doubt he would do that if
you asked him; only he would have to return
in the beginning of February, when Parliament
reassembles, you know. Do you really want
to go abroad for the winter?'

'I think I do; but I am sure that, if I went
to Cannes or Nice, I should not want to
return in the beginning of February. It

seems to be a most inconvenient thing to be a member of the British Parliament, and I wish Douglas would resign his membership. But perhaps such a sacrifice would be too heavy a one to require of him ?'

'It certainly would, unless he is a much greater fool than I take him for,' answered Peggy bluntly. 'No man, except an absolute fool, would think of sacrificing his whole career for the sake of giving his wife a few months of amusement; and supposing that any sane man did make such a fool of himself, his wife would be the very first person to despise him.'

'*C'est selon*,' observed the Countess with a smile; 'for my own part, I should never despise a man who was capable of making a great sacrifice. Some men, you know, love things, while others—but, of course, not a great many—love people. I was curious to discover in which class you would place my husband, and I find that your impression is much the same as mine. Still, there can be no telling until he has been put to the test.'

'I can't believe,' exclaimed Peggy, with rather more warmth, perhaps, than the occa-

sion warranted, 'that you would be so selfish
as to test him in that way.'

'Oh, I am selfish enough for anything.
But we will talk about something else now,
for I see that I am displeasing you; and if I
have a right to try my husband's patience, I
have none at all to try yours. Thank you for
answering my question so explicitly.'

Peggy was not conscious of having done
anything of the sort, but she was conscious of
having expressed herself with somewhat uncalled-for vehemence; and, although she was
a perfect-tempered woman, she would have
liked very well, at that moment, to box her
hostess's ears. That being a method of
showing disapproval which is precluded by
modern usages, she took refuge in distant,
good-humoured politeness for the next five
minutes, after which she got up and said
good-bye.

After her departure the Countess sat for
a long time gazing idly at the fire. She had
succeeded to some extent in discomfiting Miss
Rowley, but she was not particularly elated
by that easy triumph, and the remembrance
of a few observations which had fallen from
Peggy depressed her. 'A man who may

always be relied upon to behave like a gentleman, and who will always do what is sensible, and respectable and ordinary,' she murmured—'oh, that describes him to the life, no doubt, and it is a thousand pities that two people who were made for each other should have been separated by a person who seems to have been made only for herself. If he loved me, or if my baby had lived——'

Her eyes suddenly filled with tears; but she was not much given to weeping, and she brushed them impatiently away. 'After all,' she exclaimed, as she started up from her chair, 'it is not a question of a tragedy—who could construct a tragedy out of such materials? The real danger is that it may degenerate into a farce, and that he and I may agree to grow old and fat together quite comfortably upon the mutual understanding that nothing in this world is of genuine consequence except material well-being and political mediocrity.'

Now, there really was not, and in her heart she must have known that there was not, much risk of such a descent into bathos as that ; yet she chose to take measures for guarding against it. When Douglas returned,

she favoured him with an account of the
above-recorded conversation, which distressed
him but did not provoke him to anger.

'I dare say Peggy doesn't always choose
her words as carefully as she might,' he remarked; 'still, she seems to have been sub-
stantially in the right. It is true that, if you
insisted upon it, I would apply for the Chiltern
Hundreds, and I suppose it is equally true
that you won't insist upon it.'

'Perfectly true,' answered the Countess
rather wearily; 'and that is just why you
and I find ourselves in a *cul-de-sac*. What
does one do when one can neither advance
nor stand still? Doesn't one retrace one's
steps?'

'Only that is impossible, Hélène.'

'Not so impossible as you think, perhaps.
Shall I tell you of two things which are really
impossible? One of them is that I should
ever become reconciled to the kind of existence
which I am now leading, and the other is that
you should ever become reconciled to any
different kind of existence. It is a great
pity, but there is no help for it; so, instead
of casting stones at one another, we will go
and dress for dinner.'

By dinner-time her mood had undergone so complete a change that Douglas judged it best not to revert to the discussion of painful dilemmas. He was willing to grant any reasonable demand, as well as a good many which might fairly be accounted unreasonable, on his wife's part; but he did not think himself bound to anticipate the latter, and he had a strong impression that she was not serious in all her assertions. It was not surprising that she found life at Stoke Leighton a dull business, now that she would no longer hunt. Well, then, they must take a run abroad, that was all, and see what change of scene would do for her.

He did not at once make his benevolent intention known, because a great political gathering, at which it behoved him to be present, was to take place in the county during the ensuing week, and he was afraid that she would urge him to shirk it; but upon the eve of this important affair he announced that immediately after its conclusion he would be ready to proceed to any Southern winter station which she might select, and he was not a little disappointed by her cool reception of the proposal.

'Until the first of February, I suppose?' she said interrogatively.

'Well, I might pair, of course; but I am not sure that I should be able to manage it. Besides, to tell you the truth, Hélène, I want to be in the House during the early part of the session. If it wouldn't bore you to listen to a short dissertation upon contemporary politics, I could explain why.'

'Oh, but I think it would bore me very much,' answered the Countess, laughing. 'Almost as much, perhaps, as it would bore you to spend a whole winter in the South. Half a winter won't do, thank you; one must be born English to admit that half a loaf is better than no bread. Nevertheless, I am sincerely obliged to you for offering me the most that you can, and, as I am not going to accept this favour, I dare say you will be good enough to grant me a smaller one in its place. Will you make my excuses to Lord and Lady Winkfield, and say that I am too unwell to stay with them? I cannot flatter myself that they will miss me, and, if I went, I should only offend them by declining to face a torrent of oratory.'

Lord Winkfield was a great territorial

magnate, under whose auspices the political
gathering above mentioned was to be held,
and Douglas knew very well that offence
would be given and taken by the Countess
Radna's refusal at the last moment to join
his lordship's house-party. But, as she remained unmoved by his representations and
entreaties, he resigned himself to the snubs
which undoubtedly awaited him and set off to
fulfil his engagement without her.

He was duly snubbed by Lady Winkfield
on his arrival; but his host, who was a good-
humoured old personage, let him off with a
mild caution against allowing himself to be
hen-pecked, and he spoke so well at the
different meetings to which he was conducted
that, what with the applause of his audiences
and the congratulations of his colleagues, he
had almost got the better of his chagrin by
the evening of the second day. Having now
done all that was required of him, he took
leave of his entertainers and arranged to
make an early start on the morrow. However, he did not start so early but that his
letters were delivered to him just as he was
leaving for the station ; and amongst these
was one from his wife, the contents of which

filled him with amazement and consternation.

It was dated from London, and stated, in a
brief, matter-of-course way, that the writer
was about to cross over to Paris, *en route*
for the Riviera.

'Pray excuse this precipitation,' she added.
'It is just possible, though I fear it is not
very likely, that you may understand how
much simpler it is to cut a knot than to
exhaust one's patience and hurt one's fingers
in a vain attempt to unfasten it. For a day
or two, or even a week or two, you will feel
angry; but I am quite sure you will not feel
lonely while you have your mother and your
unmarried sister, and, above all, your Miss
Peggy, at hand to console you.'

CHAPTER XV.

IT is not unlikely that the Countess would have been pleased, and it is certain that she would have been amused, if she could have seen the effe.t produced upon her husband by the short missive which she had addressed to him. Douglas, while driving to the station, read her letter over half a dozen times without being able to arrive at the faintest comprehension of its meaning. Hélène explained nothing; she assigned no reason for her abrupt departure, nor did she mention for how long a time she proposed to absent herself; he would have supposed that she expected him to follow her had not that hypothesis been excluded by her allusion to his probable wrath and possible loneliness.

At all events, he must follow her without

loss of time ; that was the first thing that
became clear to him through a mist of total
bewilderment ; and the next was that he must
take measures to protect her from the vexa-
tious consequences to which so hasty and ill-
advised a step on her part might have laid
her open.   With this end in view he was careful, when he reached home, to avoid gratifying the evident curiosity of the servants.
He merely gave orders for such clothes as
he required to be packed up, saying that he
was about to join the Countess, who had had
to leave for the Continent rather earlier than
had been anticipated, and that he would write
or telegraph as soon as he should be able to
name a date for his return.   Then he travelled
up to London, and, crossing by the night
mail, arrived at the Gare du Nord on the
following morning.

He was tolerably confident of finding his
wife in Paris, for he knew what her customary
methods of moving from place to place were,
and that such arrangements as she deemed
essential for a long journey cannot be made
from one moment to another ; but he preferred
engaging a room at one of the large hotels to
proceeding straight to her house, and it was

not until after mid-day that he presented himself in the Avenue Friedland. It struck him
as a good omen that he was instantly and
deferentially admitted by the urbane functionary whose duty it had been, once upon a
time, to turn him away from the door. 'She
does expect me, then, after all,' he thought.
But he was not quite so well pleased when,
on entering the ante-room, he found his
further progress barred by the burly form of
Dr. Schott, nor did he half like the grin with
which his old enemy greeted him.

'I had no idea that you were in Paris, Dr.
Schott,' said he. 'May I ask whether you are
here by appointment, or only by a—happy
accident?'

'I was telegraphed for, and I have come,'
replied the Doctor, with something very like a
chuckle. 'I am always at the orders of the
Countess. But you, dear sir—I think you
have not been telegraphed for, eh? No, no!
it would be a little too soon for that.'

Douglas presumed that the man intended to
be impertinent, and was very nearly telling
him so, but restrained himself. 'You must
be aware,' he remarked, 'that my wife has
left England quite unexpectedly, and without

having given me any warning of her departure; therefore you won't be surprised at my
having come here as quickly as I could in
order to see her. Perhaps you will be so good
as to let her know that I have arrived.'

'I am not at all surprised,' the Doctor
answered, with the same ill-concealed air of
amused satisfaction, 'and the Countess shall
certainly be informed that you are desirous of
speaking with her. As for her consenting to
see you, that is another matter. Indeed, I am
by no means sure that I ought not to forbid
an interview.'

' To forbid it ?'

' In my capacity of the Countess's physician,
bien entendu ; I pretend to no other authority
over her, or I should have exerted it long ago.
If I did not fear to offend you, Mr. Colborne,
I would take the liberty to observe that you
and she did not know what you were doing
when you agreed in such a hurry to bind yourselves together. By this time you have probably discovered the difference between dreams
and realities. The Countess, at least, appears
to have made the discovery and to have been
a good deal agitated by it. All that is no
business of mine, you say? Well, sir, it is

my business—and I am paid for performing
it—to watch over my patient's state of health,
and I do not hesitate to say that her health
will suffer from the reproaches which, I perceive, are at the tip of your tongue. I have
prescribed the only remedy which seems to
me likely to prove of any service; that is,
complete change of surroundings and avoid-
ance of mental disturbance. Consequently,
we are to leave for Nice in a day or two. I
am not called upon to prescribe for you; but,
as a friend, I venture to suggest that you
should return home and attend to your affairs.
By May or June next, circumstances may have
become more favourable to your wishes; at
present, believe me, you will do no good either
to her or to yourself by insisting upon your
rights.'

By way of response Douglas rang the bell
and told the servant, who promptly appeared,
to announce him to the Countess. 'You may
say,' he added, 'that I wish to see her immediately.'

Dr. Schott made a deprecating gesture,
stuck his hands into his pockets and sauntered
towards the window. 'Please to take note,'
said he presently, over his shoulder, 'that if

you are received, it will be against my advice
and without my sanction.'

Douglas did not choose to gratify his tor-
mentor by any rejoinder ; and, after what
seemed to him an unnecessarily protracted
delay, the domestic re-entered the room with
a request that he would give himself the
trouble to step into the Countess's boudoir.

How well he remembered that exquisitely
furnished apartment, with its subdued light,
its Gobelins tapestries, and its faint, inde-
scribable perfume! It was into the same room
that he had been admitted on that evening
when he had first had the audacity to declare
his love, and everything connected with the
situation seemed quite oddly the same—including his own feelings. He had been
tremulous and excited then ; he found, somewhat to his vexation, that he was tremulous
and excited now. He had been resolved then
to learn his fate, once for all, and was not that
very like his present errand ? And when,
after keeping him waiting for a minute or two,
his wife made her appearance, arrayed in a tea-
gown which exhibited the latest inspiration of
the talented artist whom she employed to
design such habiliments for her, he felt as if

she had, somehow or other, ceased to be Hélène and had become once more the Countess Radna of the past. He was conscious of an utterly absurd access of timidity which no doubt, caused him to speak a shade more sharply than he would have done if she had looked less cool and unconcerned.

'May I ask what all this means,' he began. 'You will admit that I am entitled to some explanation, and as yet you have given me none.'

'Haven't I?' returned the Countess, ensconcing herself in a comfortable chair; 'I thought I had; but it is true that I wrote in rather a hurry. Indeed, the hurry is the only thing that demands explanation, I suppose, and I should have thought that it would explain itself. Surely a moment of reflection might have spared you the fatigue of this long journey. You know how I detest useless discussions, and you must have known (because I told you) that I had made up my mind to escape from Stoke Leighton. It is all very well to hesitate until one's mind is made up; but when once the feat has been accomplished, the sooner one acts the better. I am sorry if I have scandalized the county;

only, as I shall never return there, the question of whether these good people are scandalized or not is scarcely of so much importance to me as it is to you. However, you will be able to calm their minds a little by assuring them that I have run away alone; for Dr. Schott, I presume, doesn't count.'

'Are you speaking seriously when you say that you will never return?' asked Douglas, with a slight quiver in his voice. 'I can hardly believe that you are, because that would imply that you wish to separate yourself from me altogether.'

'Which would, of course, be inconceivable. Well, if you will excuse me, I would rather not enter upon that question just at present. I am tired and worried, and Dr. Schott will have told you that I am ill. Still, I don't mind saying positively and definitely that nothing would induce me to repeat the experiment of residing at Stoke Leighton; one failure of that description is enough for me, and I suppose you won't dispute the indisputable fact that I have failed.'

Douglas did not attempt so hopeless a task; for, indeed, there was no denying that his wife had failed to adapt herself to the conditions of English country life. He only remarked, somewhat grimly :

'Stoke Leighton is my home.'

'It is your home if you choose to make it so ; but it cannot be mine. *À la rigueur* I could put up with London, although I strongly suspect that London and you, when you are there, would get on as well as possible without me. Suppose you were to return home now and try getting on without me ? I shall be surprised as well as flattered if, after the warm weather sets in again, I receive a pressing invitation to rejoin you.'

'I can't understand what you mean,' said Douglas despairingly. 'I may be very stupid ; but I frankly confess that I am at my wits' end. What have I done that you should speak to me in this way ?'

The Countess sighed impatiently.

'What have you done ?' she echoed. 'Will you be satisfied if I answer that you have done an excessively stupid thing in rushing after me ? No, of course you won't. You are—pray forgive my candour—too *bourgeois* in your ideas to realize the wisdom of letting a wilful woman have her way or to comprehend that nothing is more ordinary than for the wife of a public man to spend the winter abroad, while his duties retain him at home; you must needs treat yourself to the luxury of one of those noisy scandals which are so dear to your countymen and countrywomen. Very well; since you will have it so, you shall not be defrauded by me of your queer, insular method of enjoying yourself. Let it be agreed and proclaimed, if you choose, that our separation is to be permanent.'

'But, in the name of reason and common-sense, why?' exclaimed Douglas, growing a little warm — for, after all, he was not a *bourgeois*, and he did not much relish being called by that name. 'Is it only because you don't like Stoke Leighton that you talk so coolly of abandoning me? That would be too absurd! Come, Hélène, won't you give me your true motives? Upon my word of honour, I am as completely in the dark about them as a man can be.'

'Your word of honour,' observed the Countess, smiling, 'is not much more to the purpose than your invocation of reason and common-sense. If you haven't discovered by this time how little reason and common-sense have to do with me or my actions, you may

well be in the dark ! I despair of being able
to enlighten you; all I can say is, that you
had better go home and allow me to go to
Nice. In fact, I shall go to Nice, whether
you allow me or not.'

Douglas paced up and down the room three
or four times before trusting himself to make
any rejoinder. He was aware that he had
reached an important crisis in his life ; he was
aware that, unless he could exert his marital
authority now, he would never be able to
exert it again; yet he shrank from issuing a
positive order. His wife, who was pecuniarly
independent of him, could not be forced to
obey his orders, nor could he emphazise them
by anything short of an ultimatum, which
appeared to have no terrors for her. He
might, as every unconcerned spectator will
perceive, have conquered by throwing himself
at her feet and repeating some of those vows
of unalterable love to which she had once lent
a willing ear ; but as he was by no means
unconcerned, and as he was very excusably
incensed, the notion of stooping to conquer
did not enter into his head. So, as soon as he
felt cool enough to measure his words deliberately, he said:

'You force me to the conclusion that you wish to rid yourself altogether of my control. I don't know, and you refuse to tell me, what has induced you to take a step for which I was utterly unprepared ; but for some time past I have not been so blind as to ignore what I suppose you meant to be obvious— that any love you may once have had for me has worn itself out. However much that may hurt me, I don't personally consider it a sufficient reason for practically annulling our marriage ; but your views of marriage are not, I know, the same as mine, and I need scarcely say that I have no wish to insist upon my rights as a husband against your will. At the same time, I think we must do one thing or the other. I can't see my way to accepting a partial separation.'

'Then we will call it a total separation, and say no more about it,' returned the Countess, with a faint flush upon her cheeks, but with an air of undiminished amiability. 'You express yourself in such admirable Christian terms that I am sure you won't hesitate to throw the whole blame upon such a heathen as me, and you are most heartily welcome to do so. Let it be assumed that the mistake

from first to last has been my fault ; it isn't
my fault that civilized nations are not civilized enough to wipe out mistakes of that
kind by means of a divorce. However, I can
at least promise to give you no trouble for the
future, and I won't detain you any longer for
the present. As you have heard from Dr.
Schott, I am not very well to-day ; so, if you
want to make formal conditions and provisos
and to have them set down in writing—as
you probably do—perhaps you wouldn't mind
calling again to-morrow.'

She was out of the room before Douglas
had time to reply ; but in truth he would
have made no reply beyond a curt acquiescence to her, had she seen fit to wait for one.
His pain and bewilderment were thrown into
the background by his just indignation ; and
as he tramped back towards the hotel in which
he was lodging, with his chin in the air and a
steady frown upon his brow, the very last
thing that he dreamt of was that his wife was
at that same moment crying her eyes out in
her bedroom because—to borrow the amaz-
ingly inappropriate phrase which she used in
her self-communings—he had 'deserted' her.

CHAPTER XVI.

THAT Douglas Colborne did well to be angry —or, at least, that he had the best ostensible reasons for being angry — everyone will admit ; but it must be also admitted that he ought to have had wit enough to perceive the extreme improbability of his wife's having behaved as she had done out of sheer caprice or impatient weariness of his society. After a dim fashion he did perceive this ; capricious as she was, and weary of him as he believed her to be, it nevertheless seemed unlikely that she should go the length of so abruptly demanding a separation without having taken the trouble to provide herself with some sort of plausible excuse. Still, the answer to that was that, likely or unlikely, the thing had happened ; and when he went to bed, after a long and very unhappy evening, he could not see his way to making any overtures for a possible reconciliation.

Of course, matters presented themselves to him under a somewhat different aspect on the ensuing morning — matters always do look different in the morning ; and that is one of the many objections to answering disagreeable letters by return of post. Douglas awoke to the full consciousness of having been disagreeably dealt with ; but a shave and a cold bath aided him to the conclusion that he himself had not been precisely agreeable. Like the honest man that he was, he did his best to comprehend his wife's standpoint, and although he could not, as a matter of fact, comprehend it in the least, he advanced far enough on the way towards doing so to acknowledge that she had not met with all the consideration to which she was entitled at his hands. He ought to have remembered that some allowance should be made for feminine vagaries and eccentricities ; he ought to have seen that to a woman of her class and habits Stoke Leighton, with its provincial sports and its long days of solitude, must needs end by becoming intolerable ; he ought, perhaps, to have replied to her first remonstrances by promising to take her to the South, and even, if she made a point of it, to leave her there for a month or two by herself. As a rule, the wives of English squires consider it a part of their duty to be where their husbands are ; but, then, his wife was not an ordinary English squire's wife, and he should have borne that circumstance in mind in his dealings with her. Upon the whole, his conscience would not permit him to shirk the obligation of making a sort of apology. He did not propose to make a very full or a very abject apology, because he conceived that something in the shape of an apology was due also to him ; but he was anxious to put himself in the right, and he was not sure that he had done this on the previous afternoon. According to the popular saying, it takes two to make a quarrel, and he was resolved not to quarrel with Hélène ; although she could, no doubt, if she persisted in her present attitude, force him to separate himself from her. There is a shade of distinction between acquiescence and consent.

It was in the admirably calm and unimpassioned frame of mind induced by these

reflections that he had himself driven once
more to the Avenue Friedland and was again
ushered into the anteroom where he had held
his parley with Dr. Schott. This time, however, it was not the Doctor, but the Baroness
von Bickenbach, who advanced to greet him,
and the Baroness wagged her head mourn-
fully, as well as reproachfully, while she took
his outstretched hand.

'Ah, monsieur,' she sighed, 'what a misfortune ! what a sad misfortune !'

'It is a misfortune which may be repaired,
I hope,' answered Douglas, in his halting
French. 'Indeed, it is not so much a misfortune as a misunderstanding. If I have been
in any way to blame for it, I am ready to beg
pardon, and I have come here to say so.
Would you, if it is not troubling you too
much, be so good as to inform my wife that
I have come ?'

'Oh,' returned the Baroness, with another
deep sigh, 'there is no need to inform her.
She knew very well that you would come, and
everything has been prepared. As for begging
her pardon, I do not wish to discourage
you, but I fear that it is too late to do that
now. She would never have sent for me

if she had not meant to break with you finally.'

'She may be induced to reconsider her decision,' observed Douglas, choking down an inclination to retort that he was the Countess's husband, not her slave, and that he might fairly claim to have a voice in any decision that might recommend itself to her.

'She may,' agreed the Baroness despondently; 'but, alas! I doubt whether she will be induced to do so by you or by me. You do not know her, or you would never have suffered things to come to their present pass. Do you remember that day when you stopped me in the street, and when I cautioned you about her, and advised you to go home? I thought at the time that she would refuse you, as she had refused so many others; and I believe she did refuse you. I was very sorry, for your sake, when you joined us afterwards in the Pyrenees. She accepted you then under the influence of excitement and emotion; I do not think she would have accepted you if it had not been for that unlucky thunderstorm.'

'In short, you do not think that she ever cared for me.'

'I will not say that. She did care for you, and you might have made her care for you to the end of your life; only——' The Baroness paused, and muttered some ejaculation in German. 'It is difficult to explain,' she resumed presently, 'especially when one is not speaking in one's own language; but I think that you have had your opportunity, and that you have missed it. Ah, monsieur, pardon me for saying so; but you must have been very—*maladroit.*'

The censure was, perhaps, not wholly unmerited. Douglas received it very meekly; yet he remained of opinion that clumsiness is not an offence beyond reach of pardon, and that love, if it has once existed, cannot be killed quite so easily as the Baroness seemed to imply. He was beginning to formulate these modest views when he was interrupted by the entrance of Dr. Schott, who drew his heels together and saluted the visitor with a profound bow.

'I am instructed,' announced the Doctor, in his thick, harsh voice, the accents of which betrayed some inward exultation, 'to treat with you, sir, on behalf of the Countess Radna. She is still, I regret to say, indisposed, and does not feel equal to the discussion of matters of business; although I am to tell you that, as soon as we have concluded our little talk, she will not object to see you in my presence and that of the Baroness von Bickenbach, should you desire it.'

'I desire to see my wife alone,' said Douglas, 'and I may have to insist upon doing so. That, however, is a question between her and me, with which you are in no way concerned. What about the matters of business which you say you are charged to discuss with me? They won't entail a great deal of discussion, I hope?'

The Doctor bowed, and replied that he hoped they wouldn't. 'Indeed,' he added, 'there is no reason why they should; for the Countess's conditions are in some respects so moderate and in others so liberal that they can scarcely fail to be acceptable to you. First of all, I am instructed to say that a sum of money large enough to produce an income of at least three thousand pounds sterling will at once be placed to your credit, and that, if you find that donation insufficient, it will be increased. Secondly——'

' Stop a moment,' interrupted Douglas. ' I

should have thought it would have been understood—but as it apparently isn't understood, I may as well say so—that, in the event of a separation being agreed upon, I shall not dream of touching a penny of my wife's fortune. Now you can go on.'

The Doctor inclined his head and obeyed. The remainder of the stipulations were such as might have been anticipated, and, when summed up, amounted to a declaration of complete independence, modified by certain concessions which seemed to have been framed with a view to averting scandal. It was suggested, for instance, that the husband and wife should for the future meet once or twice in the course of the year, as friends, and that the fact of their union having been dissolved by mutual consent should not be formally made public.

Douglas did not again break in upon Dr. Schott's harangue; but when it appeared to have come to an end, he said: 'I have no remark to make about all that, except that I must decline to be placed in the ridiculous position of meeting my wife as a friend, and that I see no object at all in keeping up a pretence which everybody would know to be a pretence. But I will explain myself to her, not to you. Now that you have discharged your mission, be so kind as to go and tell her from me that no arrangement of any sort can be concluded until I have had a few words with her in private.'

'I will deliver your message, sir,' answered the Countess's plenipotentiary, speaking with that exaggerated deference which is almost as pleasant to the person addressed as a slap in the face; 'but I have already had the honour of mentioning to you what my instructions are upon the subject.'

He was absent only for a short time, during which Bickenbach continued to emit noisy sighs at regular intervals, like minute-guns, and when he re-entered the room he was accompanied by the Countess, who looked perfectly serene and composed. She walked straight up to her husband, and held out her hand to him, with a smile, saying:

'*Sans rancune, n'est-ce pas?*' And then, before he could reply, she added: 'I am glad you won't take the money. The offer had to be made as a matter of form, you understand; but it was not intended to be insulting, and I felt tolerably sure that you would not take advantage of it. I am capable of doing you justice, you see, now that our relations have been placed upon a less impossible footing.'

Douglas was a good deal disconcerted. He did not perceive that this assumption of good-humoured sang-froid must necessarily, at such a moment, be a mere mask, and that, whatever might be his wife's feelings, they could not be those which she professed. On the contrary, his conviction was that, for good or for ill, she had resolved to be done with him; that, to use Bickenbach's words, he had had his opportunity and missed it, and that nothing which he could do or say now would avail to piece together the fragments of two shattered lives. Not, for the matter of that, that the Countess's life seemed to be in much danger of being shattered. Her marriage had been a painful episode, the memory of which she would doubtless hasten to put away from her, now that she had regained her freedom; after all, it was but logical that she should so regard a tie which for her had no religious sanction or significance. Then, too, while she stood smiling at him, he was sensible once more of that remoteness from her which had vexed him on the previous day, and which, in spite of himself, caused him to speak drily and formally. However, he made his little effort.

'I came here to ask your pardon, Hélène,' he began. 'On thinking things over, I saw that you had some reasons for complaint against me ; I wished to tell you that I was sorry for having shown any want of consideration for your wishes, and that, although I still thought you had taken a most extreme and uncalled-for way of manifesting your displeasure, I should be willing, on my side, to overlook that and let bygones be bygones. That, in the main, was what I intended to say ; but it stands to reason that I could say a good deal more if you would consent to see me alone for a few minutes. Is that too great a favour to ask ?'

'All things considered, you have been so docile and so accommodating,' answered the Countess, with a slightly mocking intonation, 'that I can refuse you nothing ; and, if you make a point of it, I will request our good friends here to leave us. At the same time, I must warn you that the solitude of the Sahara would not bring us any nearer to one another than we are now. As far as pardon goes, I assure you that I do not cherish the smallest feeling of bitterness against you, though I regret to hear from Dr. Schott that you decline to be my friend. The truth is that you are absolutely pardonable in some respects, and absolutely unpardonable in others. To the best of my belief, you deserve neither credit nor blame; we are what we are—all of us— and we cannot make ourselves what we are not. That is why we are going to part, you and I, and that is why anything in the shape of a parting scene seems to me to be super-fluous. As you please, however.'

What answer could be made to such a speech? Douglas was hurt and stung by it into rejoining: 'Any scene that you consider superfluous must be rendered superfluous by that fact alone. There is nothing more to be said, that I know of, except of course that the money which you were kind enough to bestow upon my sister at the time of her marriage must now be returned to you. I will see to it as soon as I reach home again.'

'Let me beg of you to do nothing of the sort —or, rather, since you do not seem to be in a mood to grant concessions, let me point out to you that you and your sister are two distinct

persons. I have no quarrel with her ; nor, I
hope, has she any with me. At all events, if my
humble wedding-present is to be flung back in
my face, it must be flung by her hand or her
husband's, not by yours. There is to be a
quarrel between you and me, since you insist
upon calling it by that name; but I trust that
this will not disturb my amicable relations
with your family when I return to London, if
I ever do return to London. And, now that
I come to think of it, I have a house there.
Are you, I wonder, cool enough to realize the
immense advantage, from your own point of
view, of washing our matrimonial dirty linen
in secret ?'

'I am afraid I cannot pretend to be as cool
as you are,' answered Douglas ; ' still, I think
I may safely say that no degree of subsequent
coldness will ever reconcile me to the idea that
my sister is drawing a large income from one
who refuses to be my wife any longer. I
shall tell her what my notion of her obvious
duty is, and I imagine that she will concur in
it ; but, as you truly say, I am not in a position to issue commands. As for what you
elegantly call washing our dirty linen in
secret, I need hardly tell you that I shall not

condescend to secrecy. I am not ashamed of
myself, and I am not going to behave as
though I were.'

The Countess gazed at him compassion-
ately. ' Poor fellow !' she ejaculated ; ' what
a hornets' nest you are about to stir up !
You will outlive the annoyance, though, and
you will have the comfort of pluming yourself
upon your perfect integrity. After all, I
don't know why I should pity you.'

Pity was certainly the very last thing that
her husband was desirous of claiming from
her. He left her presence and her house a
few minutes later, and it cannot be denied
that his mingled distress and anger were to
some extent allayed by that consciousness of
integrity to which she had referred. He had
done all that he could possibly do ; he had
gone as far as any human being with an
atom of self-respect could go in condoning an
offence which he had every right to resent
and craving forgiveness for offences of which,
when all was said, he had not been intention-
ally guilty. It only remained for him to seek
oblivion in the pursuit of an honourable
career and to take care that he did not break
his heart for the sake of one who assuredly

was unworthy of so tragic a tribute to her fascinations.

Thus hastily was terminated an alliance which, perhaps, had been contracted with undue haste ; and thus, in all probability, would a thousand alliances terminate, were there a thousand ladies whose marriage vows weighed as lightly upon them as did those of the Countess Radna. Naturally, Mrs. Colborne was not a lady of that description ; and deeply grieved and shocked was she when her son appeared unexpectedly in Elvaston Place one evening with the intelligence of the catastrophe which had come upon him.

'This is much too dreadful to be possible !' was the comment which at once rose to her lips ; and the next thing that she said was just what Douglas had felt sure that she would say : ' I do hope you haven't told anybody else !'

He replied that he had not as yet done so, because he had seen nobody else to speak to, since his arrival in England, except a railway-porter, a cabman and a butler ; ' but,' he added, ' I have no intention of concealing the truth, though I am not bound to proclaim it. There would be no object in a concealment

which, at the best, could only be temporary;
for dreadful as you may think my separation
from my wife, and dreadful as I myself think
it, it is an accomplished fact. Our union
could not be more completely dissolved if one
of us were dead.'

It took some little time to persuade Mrs.
Colborne of the truth of the latter assertion ;
and even when she seemed to be persuaded,
she had certain mental reservations, resolving
that she would write to her daughter-in-law
and explain that Douglas was hereditarily
undemonstrative, that his affections were all
the more deep and steady because he seldom
gave verbal expression to them, and so forth.
Meanwhile, she was very pleased to hear that
the Countess did not wish to quarrel with her,
and she dissented altogether from her son's
quixotic notion that Phyllis ought at once to
surrender the dowry upon the strength of
which she had espoused a man of small
means.

Colonel and Mrs. Percy were quite of one
mind with her as to that, and were not unnaturally indignant with Douglas for having
so selfishly placed them in a delicate position.
Some subsequent correspondence passed be-

tween them and the Countess upon the
subject, and they did, in a half-hearted sort of
way, offer to submit to the suggested sacrifice ; but, of course, the upshot of it was that
they kept the money, while they conceived a
grudge against the head of the Colborne
family which, for the matter of that, they
continue to harbour at the present day.

Douglas, indeed, obtained very little sympathy from his relatives. The hero of a total
fiasco cannot expect to be sympathized with,
and a man who, after marrying one of the
greatest heiresses and most charming women
in Europe, is unable to induce her to live
with him must be admitted to have made a
very bad kind of fiasco. His sister Loo was
the only one who was really sorry for him,
and condoled with him honestly, if a trifle
clumsily.

'Ah,' she exclaimed one day, 'what a
thousand pities it is that you didn't marry
Peggy Rowley! Peggy wouldn't have picked
quarrels with you ; she wouldn't have wanted
to drag you abroad in the middle of the hunting season ; she would have gone to church,
like other people, and she would have taken
an interest in the things that interest you.

But it's too late to think of all that now !'

It was much too late to think of it, and not very good taste to speak of it. Such was the substance of Douglas's rejoinder; nevertheless, he could not help inwardly acknowledging that there was a good deal of truth in what his sister said. Not that it signified; because he did not love Peggy Rowley, whereas, in spite of all that had happened, he did still love his wife.

END OF VOL. I.

BILLING AND SONS, PRINTERS, GUILDFORD.